SEBASTIAN BARRY

A THOUSAND MOONS

A Novel

faber

First published in 2020
by Faber & Faber Limited
Bloomsbury House
74–77 Great Russell Street
London WC1B 3DA
This paperback edition first published in 2021

Typeset by Faber & Faber Limited
Printed and bound by CPI Group (UK) Ltd, Croydon, CR0 4YY

A CIP record for this book
is available from the British Library

ISBN 978–0–571–33339–4

2 4 6 8 10 9 7 5 3 1

A Thousand Moons

Sebastian Barry was born in Dublin in 1955. The current Laureate for Irish Fiction, his novels have twice won the Costa Book of the Year award, the Independent Booksellers Award and the Walter Scott Prize. He had two consecutive novels shortlisted for the Man Booker Prize, *A Long Long Way* (2005) and the top ten bestseller *The Secret Scripture* (2008), and has also won the Kerry Group Irish Fiction Prize, the Irish Book Awards Novel of the Year and the James Tait Black Memorial Prize. He lives in County Wicklow.

Further praise for *A Thousand Moons*:

'Like all of Barry's wounded and yet strong characters, [Winona] is rendered truly human and complex by his writing: a mixture of innocence and bravery, and another unforgettable character deftly sewn into the tapestry of an Irish family who would never regard her as part of their story. Barry superbly brings her into his compelling, expansive and humane fictional universe.' Dermot Bolger, *Sunday Post*

'Lyrical and mesmerising . . . [the] story is told with compassion and a keen eye for all facets of the human condition. A thrilling return.' Doug Johnstone, *Big Issue*

'Distinguished above all by the remarkable power of its narrator's voice . . . Winona is a wonderful creation.' *Literary Review*

'With his lyrical prose, Barry brings vividly to life a society struggling with violence and disorder . . . and the strength of love and friendship that can be found, in sometimes unexpected places. In returning readers to a world they already know, sequels rarely quite match the freshness and surprise of a brand-new story; nevertheless, people who loved *Days Without End* are unlikely to be disappointed.' *i*

'Barry's prose is as evocative and lyrical as ever and his themes of us versus them have a strong resonance today, especially when it comes to the othering or perceived outsiders.' *The Crack*

'Anybody who has read, or heard, even a whit of Sebastian Barry, novelist and playwright, will know that the man can make prose sing . . . A book of lyrical beauty, shot through with savagery and an empathy for those who feel, for whatever reason – race, religion, sex – that they don't fit into this world.' Donal O'Donoghue, *RTÉ Guide*

'Vivid, enthralling . . . *A Thousand Moons* is a tale graced with such a glow of love that even the most hopeless circumstances seem burnished with hope.' Huston Gilmore, *Daily Express*

'Thrilling and beautifully written.' *Psychologies Magazine*

'A richly poetic read. Barry is concerned again with shifting sexual, personal and political boundaries, with the effects of tumultuous times – of rivalry, lawlessness and fissure – on individuals, families and communities, and with interactions between those on opposite sides of a political debate.' Lucy Atkins, *Sunday Times*

'Strange and beautiful . . . spine-tingling.' *Mail on Sunday*

'Barry's lyrical and narrative skills are beyond question, and he paints a vivid picture of a land unsettled . . . His message is that love – in its many forms – conquers all, but even this apparent truism is tempered by the realisation that while "even mournful folk could borrow" from it, it is "a mortgaged joy".' *Hot Press*

'Instinctively, Barry understands that stories speak loudest when they speak only for themselves, when they make no grand claims for universality or decisiveness . . . *A Thousand Moons* is not a narrative stretched across the frame of a treatise, it is Winona's story, rendered with dignity in jewel-studded prose. Readers will be hard pressed to find three finer sentences than the last of this novel. It is an end befitting a book whose titular premise is there is no end.' *Weekend Australian*

'This is a subtle, troubling novel, full of silences, full of pain . . . Barry knows that it is too much to look for redemption in a story like Winona's, but in his telling he shows that love offers at least a spark of hope.' Erica Wagner, *Financial Times*

'Barry is a master at creating a mesmerising voice that commands your undivided attention, and filling a landscape so skilfully it feels like a place you already know . . . Barry fills every margin of the page with emotion and imagination. Very quickly you forget you are reading fiction and believe it is the very truth.' Rosemary Goring, *The Herald*

'Unmissable . . . extraordinary.' *Bookseller*

'One of Sebastian Barry's extraordinary gifts as a writer is his boundless capacity for empathy, for inhabiting the skin, nerves and mouths of characters the river of history tends to wash away . . . This attention to the stories of individual figures within broader generations has created a humane and textured history of the Irish nation and its emigrant experiences.' Susan Cahill, *Irish Times*

'Barry is the Laureate for Irish Fiction, but he is also the laureate of empathy . . . The denouement in *A Thousand Moons* is heartbreaking, and elegiac. In a prayer-like appeal, Winona leaves us with words which address self-hood, identity, freedom and love. "That I had souls that loved me and hearts that watched over me was a truth self-evident to hold." And that from the smithy of Barry's imagination she could be talking to us right here, right now, is an extraordinary achievement.' Paul Perry, *Sunday Independent* (*Ireland*)

'[Winona's] adventures take her on a journey that is horrifying, thrilling and enchanting in equal measure, all of it rendered in Barry's uniquely lyrical prose, which seems at once effortless and dense with meaning. This novel, like its predecessor, provides a compelling answer to those who claim that authors should stick to their own when it comes to telling stories . . . prose this good is a kind of enchantment, transcending the constructs that are supposed to define us to speak in a voice that is truly universal.' Alex Preston, *Observer*

by the same author

fiction

THE WHEREABOUTS OF ENEAS MCNULTY
ANNIE DUNNE
A LONG LONG WAY
THE SECRET SCRIPTURE
ON CANAAN'S SIDE
THE TEMPORARY GENTLEMAN
DAYS WITHOUT END

plays

BOSS GRADY'S BOYS
PRAYERS OF SHERKIN
WHITE WOMAN STREET
THE ONLY TRUE HISTORY OF LIZZIE FINN
THE STEWARD OF CHRISTENDOM
OUR LADY OF SLIGO
HINTERLAND
FRED AND JANE
WHISTLING PSYCHE
THE PRIDE OF PARNELL STREET
DALLAS SWEETMAN
TALES OF BALLYCUMBER
ANDERSEN'S ENGLISH
ON BLUEBERRY HILL

poetry

THE WATER-COLOURIST
FANNY HAWKE GOES TO THE MAINLAND FOREVER
THE PINKENING BOY

To C

Sometimes even to live is an act of courage.

SENECA

Chapter One

I am Winona.

In early times I was Ojinjintka, which means rose. Thomas McNulty tried very hard to say this name, but he failed, and so he gave me my dead cousin's name because it was easier in his mouth. Winona means first-born. I was not first-born.

My mother, my elder sister, my cousins, my aunts, all were killed. They were souls of the Lakota that used to live on those old plains. I wasn't too young to remember – maybe I was six or seven – but all the same I didn't remember. I knew it happened because afterwards the soldiers brought me into the fort and I was an orphan.

A little girl can suffer many a seachange. By the time I got back to my people, I couldn't converse with them. I remember sitting in the teepee with the other women and not being able to answer them. By that time I was all of thirteen or so. After a few days I found the words again. The women rushed forward and embraced me as though I had only just arrived to them that very moment. Only when I spoke our language could they really see me. Then Thomas McNulty came to get me again and took me back to Tennessee.

Even when you come out of bloodshed and disaster in the end you have got to learn to live. You have to look about you, see how things are, grow things or buy things as the case may be.

The little town near by us in Tennessee was called Paris. Lige Magan's farm was about seven miles out. It was quite a few years after the war but the town was still full of rough Union soldiers kicking their heels, and the defeated butternut boys were a sort of secret presence, though they were not in their uniforms. Vagabonds on every little byway. And state militia watchful for those vagabonds.

It was a town of many eyes watching you anyhow, an uneasy place.

To present yourself in a dry-goods store to buy items you have got to have best English or something else happens. At the fort Mrs Neale had given me my first English words. In later times John Cole got me two books of grammar. I looked at them long and good.

It is bad enough being an Indian without talking like a raven. The white folks in Paris were not all good speakers themselves. Some were from other places. Germans, Swedes. Some were Irish like Thomas McNulty, and only got to English when they got to America.

But myself being a young Indian woman I guess I had to talk like an empress. Of course I could have offered my list of items that Rosalee Bouguereau, who worked on Lige's farm, had written out. But it was better to speak.

Else what was happening was, I was going to be beaten up every time I was in town. It was English kept me from that. Some straggly farmhand might look at you and see the dark skin and the black hair and think that gave him a right to knock you down and kick you. No one saying boo to him for that. No sheriff or deputy neither.

It wasn't a crime to beat an Indian, not at all.

John Cole, even though he had been out as a soldier and was a good farmer, got bad treatment in town because his grandmother or the woman before his grandmother was an Indian person. So that was writ in his face a little. Even English couldn't protect him. Because he was a big grown man maybe, he couldn't hope for mercy just all the time. He had a lovely face as people attested in especial Thomas McNulty but I guess the townsmen could sometimes see the Indian in it. They beat him so bad and then he was just a plank of suffering in the bed and Thomas McNulty swearing he would go in and kill someone.

But Thomas McNulty's shortcoming was he was poor. We were all poor. Lige Magan was poor enough, and he *owned* the farm, and we were poor underneath Lige.

Poor worse than Lige.

When a poor person does anything he has to do it quietly. When a poor person kills, for instance, he has got to do it very quietly and run as fast as those little deer that float out of the woods.

Also, Thomas had been in Leavenworth prison for desertion, so the uniforms about the town made him jumpy, even though he always said he loved the army.

I myself was lower than Rosalee Bouguereau. She was a black-skinned saint of a woman let me tell you. She used to go out and shoot rabbits with her brother's rifle along the back woods of Lige's farm there. In the famous battle with Tach Petrie – famous to us anyhow, when he and his accomplices had tried to rob us, advancing on our homestead with implacable intent – she distinguished herself by reloading the rifles faster than ever was – so said John Cole.

But she was a slave before the war and a slave is low down in the eyes of white folks of course.

So I was lower than that.

I was just the cinders of an Indian fire in the eyes of the town. Indians in bulk were long gone from Henry County. Cherokee. Chickasaw. Folks didn't like to see an ember drifting back.

In the eyes of the Great Mystery we were all souls alike. Trying to make our souls skinny enough to squeeze into paradise. That's what my mother said. Everything I remember of my mother is like the little pouch of things that a child carries to hold what is precious to her. When such a love is touched by Death then something deeper even than Death grows in your heart. My mother fussed over us, myself and my sister. She was interested in how fast we could run, and how high we could jump, and she never tired of telling us how pretty we were. We were just little girls, out there on the plains, under the starlight.

Thomas McNulty sometimes liked to tell me I was as pretty as the things *he* thought were pretty – roses, robins and the like. It was mother's talk he was doing since I had no mother then. It was strange that in the old wars he had killed many of my people when he was a soldier. He might have killed even some of my own family, he didn't know.

'I was too young to remember,' I would say to him. Of course I hadn't been, but it came to the same thing.

It used to make me feel very strange listening to him talk about that. I would start to burn from the centre of my body. I had my own little pearl-handled gun that the poet McSweny gave me in Grand Rapids. I could have shot Thomas with that. Sometimes I thought I *should* shoot something – shoot someone. Of course I did shoot one of Tach Petrie's men, not actually during the famous battle, but another time, when they accosted us on the road – right through the chest. And he shot me, but it was only a bruise, not a wound.

I had the wound of being a lost child. Thing was it was they that healed me, Thomas McNulty and John Cole. They had done their damnedest I guess. So they both gave me the wound and healed it, which is a hard fact in its way.

I guess I had no choice in the matter. Once your mother is taken from you you can't ever catch up with her again. You can't cry out 'Wait for me' when the winds turn cold under a wolf moon and she has walked far ahead of you across the grasses searching for wood.

So Thomas McNulty rescued me twice. The second time, as Thomas ventured back through the battlefield with me in tow, dressed as it happened as a drummer boy, Starling Carlton wanted to kill me, right there. We bumped into him. He was waving his sword and shouting. He said all the Indians had to be killed, it was the major's orders, and he was going to do just that. So Thomas McNulty had to kill him instead. Thomas was very sad about that. They had been soldiers together a long time.

I remembered all of that clearly enough.

Oftentimes as a girl I would cry for no reason. I would drift away and find a secluded spot. There I would let the tears loose and it might be so dark behind my eyes it was as if I had fallen blind. John Cole would come look for me. And he had the sense to put an arm about me and not to ask me to say anything I had no words for, English or Lakota.

John Cole. A lot of his love for me was expressed in practical things. He got me the books with grammar as I said and set to teaching me even though he hadn't too much learning himself. Not just letters but numbers too he taught me.

When Lige Magan thought I was ready he went and asked about employment with his friend the lawyer Briscoe. All that sort of work I did a good while, writing and reckoning numbers. I was so proud to do it.

The lawyer Briscoe had a fine house and a garden with flowers that didn't belong to Tennessee, roses from England mostly. He wrote a book about his roses that was printed in Memphis. It took pride of place in his office.

Ojinjintka means rose as I said. I don't know what sort of rose. Maybe a lost prairie rose.

Not a true rose like one of the lawyer Briscoe's. A rose to my people.

The lawyer Briscoe pressed on me cherished books. I carried them home and read them in the parlour by the stove. The breeze from the meadow touching and touching the pages. Those pleasant evenings when there was nothing to do only listen to Rosalee's beloved brother

Tennyson Bouguereau singing those old songs he knew. Myself sunk in thoughts. Those thoughts that books bring to mind.

Of course that was all before Jas Jonski. A boy that never read a book, come to think of it. Could barely write a letter.

1870s it all must have been, after the war, and after Thomas got home from prison. It might even have been the year that General Custer was killed. Or just before.

But all the years went by fleet of foot. Like ponies running across the endless grasses.

Chapter Two

Jas Jonski was the clerk in the dry-goods store. He worked for a miserable ghost of a man called Mr Hicks. The first time I stepped into the store, I knew he liked me.

'You John Cole's daughter,' he said, without a trace of fear.

'How you know I John Cole's daughter?' I said. For my part it was worrying even to be recognised.

He said that last fall he had brought out some heavy supplies in the wagon and he wondered that I didn't remember as he had complimented me.

'You're even prettier now,' he said, brave as you like.

I didn't know what to say to him. In its own way it was like a sudden ambush. I was ready to defend myself. Thomas McNulty said a girl had to be sure and know how to use her knife, how to use her little pistol, all that. I had a thin little steel knife also in the hem of my petticoat, if the gun failed me. It was English steel. Thomas McNulty showed me all the best places to stick in a knife if you want to stop someone.

But every time I went into town for supplies, he was pleasant to me. As if maybe there was someone in town now to trust. There was something between us but I had no name for it. It seemed a good thing. I began to look forward to seeing him and I used to hurry the mules along to get there, much to their annoyance.

Yes, Jas Jonski was very sweet on me and after six months of measuring out cane sugar for me, and all the rest, my wagon lost a wheel and he ran me out to Lige Magan's place, and got talking to Thomas McNulty. Thomas McNulty would talk to the devil so Jas Jonski had no trouble with him. So Thomas McNulty and John Cole began to know who he was. I never saw John Cole look at someone with less admiration.

But Jas Jonski was either blind or in love and he didn't seem to notice. He started to come out to the farm regular and when he found out that Thomas McNulty liked this expensive molasses that came up from New Orleans, he used to bring a pot of that sometimes. He would sit there beaming and talking, and Thomas scooping out the molasses with a twig like a bear, and John Cole scowling and saying nothing. John Cole could take or leave molasses, unless it was the cheap stuff was put into the tobacco after the harvest. Jas Jonski beaming, like a sun that just wouldn't set no matter how dark the evening.

'I like the town,' Jas Jonski said to John Cole, 'but I sure do like all this countryside too.'

John Cole didn't say anything.

The most John Cole would allow of courtship was Jas Jonski walking me ten minutes in the wood. I wasn't even allowed to hold his hand. Jas Jonski's modest ambition was to own his own store and he also talked vaguely about moving to Nashville where he had family. Not a few times he stopped and stood me in front of him and made declarations. It was exceedingly pleasant to see his face colour up with all his fervent protestations. Just like in the story books he *protested* his love.

Then Jas Jonski thought he might do well to marry me and he asked me about that. I didn't know how old I was but I guess I wasn't yet seventeen. I was born under the Full Buck Moon, that's all I knew for sure. He said he was nineteen. He was a red-haired boy with a burned-looking face all the year, not just high summer.

It was then John Cole got a red face too. Boiled up like a catfish.

'No, sir, madam,' he said.

I was working for the lawyer Briscoe after all which was an unusual occupation for a girl let alone an Indian. I think John Cole was intending me to be the first Indian president.

Well I thought I might very much like to marry Jas

Jonski. Just liked the sound of it. I could sort of see it. I had a picture of it in my mind. I hadn't even kissed him yet but I could see my face tilting up for his kiss. We had held hands when we were out of John Cole's sight.

But John Cole being a wise man saw other things. He had no rosy pictures. He knew what the world was like and what the world would say and then what the world would do. How right he was in everything mostly.

But I was nearly seventeen or maybe I was seventeen and what did I know, nothing. Well, I knew some things. Way back in my mind was a black painting with blood and screaming in it and blood bursting out. The soft bronze skin of my sister, my aunts. Sometimes I *could* remember things, or thought I could. Maybe I said I couldn't remember because I didn't want to – even to myself. Bluecoats tumbling in on top of us and bayonets and bullets and fire and souls killed in violent fashion. I don't know. Maybe it was just what Thomas McNulty told me. A blackened painting. But then the long clear memory of what Thomas McNulty and John Cole did, all the mighty efforts they made to please me and give me shelter.

Thomas McNulty wasn't a real mother but he nearly was. From time to time he would even wear a dress.

I was thinking Jas Jonski might continue on from John and Thomas, in the matter of pleasing a person, and giving shelter.

He was no particular picture of a person what with his reddened face. The whole cut of him was like the underside of a fallen log when you haul it up. Well, but, from twenty paces now I can attest he looked alright. Ah he was just an ordinary boy, a scanty boy really that came from old Poles who came over to America, but the thing that was really important about him to the people of Paris was, he was white. He was a whiteman. Now love may be blind but those townsfolk were not. Not so much.

People saying the same things to you over and over can wear you down. I knew that Mr Hicks thought Jas Jonski had gone mad. Maybe even was wicked in some way. To want to go marrying something closer to a monkey than a man, was how Mr Hicks framed it. Jas Jonski told me all this and was very angry but maybe a little affrighted also. Although Jas Jonski had a mother in Nashville I was never taken there to see her, nothing like that.

○

The day came when I got back to the farm all bruised. Rosalee Bouguereau screamed when she saw me and brought me out back to the wash-house because there was secret work to do on me that she didn't need the men to be seeing. Then she brought me into the house and mixed up a mash of leaves and gently rubbed it into my broken face.

When the men came in from the work Thomas McNulty was expostulating and grinding his teeth.

'I don't know why you ever let a little girl go into that town,' said Rosalee Bouguereau.

'Oh, hush now,' said her brother Tennyson, but even he didn't know what he meant by that. His elegant face was shrouded in fright.

It felt like my bones were all cracked in my face like a dropped plate. A few days later when I went out to plash my face in the water barrel I could see even in the shaking water that I was no picture. It was the same day I started to shake too, just like that water. I shook for two weeks, and though I stopped shaking I could aver that something in me, deep within, was shaking a long time after. Like the ricochet of a bullet, echoing in a rocky gully.

O

My marriage dress was only half sewn at that time and Thomas McNulty used to have it up on a high-backed chair, so he could reach it easily and work on it, when he had a spare hour. It looked like a person, white as a ghost.

'I don't want to be married now, best put that dress away for another time,' I said.

'Mercy me,' said Thomas, with all the anguish of the seamstress who has spent hours and hours stitching.

There was a sort of despair in the house. Like the sky had fallen and no one had the mules and the ropes to drag it back up again.

John Cole said he would go in and talk to Sheriff Flynn.

'Don't you be such a fool,' said Thomas McNulty. He said it kindly, softly.

It was just that you wanted to do something. In that world if there was a misdeed, you felt like there should be something done to balance it immediately. Justice. Even before the whitemen came I think it was like that. My mother used to tell a story about my own people hundreds of years ago. There was a band that spoke our language but that had separated out from us and they began to eat their enemies after battle. They began to come to the places where we buried our dead and eat them too, stealing the corpses away in the night. They would try and capture one of us and eat us. How I trembled to hear that story. Eventually our tribe went to war with them, and killed many. In the end the last of them were in a big cave and we set piles of wood into the mouth of it and said if they didn't stop eating people, we would light the wood. They didn't want to stop so the fire was lit. It burned for a week, deep in the mountain.

But if that was terrible to hear as a child it seemed also to speak of justice. Justice. To do something to right things immediately. You wanted to do that. Even if it meant killing. Otherwise much worse would be in line to happen. Thomas McNulty and John Cole felt it too, it was part of that world where we tried to live. They had defended the farm that time against Tach Petrie and his gang like I say who came with their guns to take the money earned from tobacco that year. They were brave as anyone that ever lived.

But we were poor and two of us were Indians.

There was no crime in hitting an Indian anyhow, as I said. Lige Magan went to the lawyer Briscoe who of course was his friend and his father's friend for affirmation of that and he affirmed it.

Lige Magan came back in dark pensive mood.

Thomas McNulty and John Cole didn't really have anything but me. I mean, that they couldn't live without. That they would give their lives for. So they said. It was terribly painful to hear them say that and then say they felt so bad that the one thing they had of such value had been injured and they didn't know what to do. And that maybe, as Lige Magan had found out, they couldn't rectify it even if they knew how.

Further west they would have just started shooting, if they could pinpoint the culprit.

Thomas McNulty wondered would there be any good in scouring up and down Paris for vagabonds and vagrants and maybe going up and down the roads hither and thither on the same mission. John Cole said that in these days the roads were nothing but vagabonds and vagrants. Thomas McNulty sighed and said they had been such themselves many is the time.

They kept asking, 'Did you even see who done it? A stray person? Someone you knew?' I kept saying, 'I don't rightly know.'

I went and stood by John Cole's leg like a dog that isn't sure if it has done wrong or right.

Because I thought I should know and wondered if I did. I did remember very vaguely struggling away and out of the town, and then stumbling along like an injured pony till I got to the lawyer Briscoe's house and Lana Jane Sugrue his housekeeper called her two brothers and they ran me home in the lawyer Briscoe's buggy. I might have been crying and I might not. The brothers, Joe and Virg, hardly dared look at me, I saw them looking at each other nervously. I remembered the fields and wastelands rushing by as they frothed up the little pony. Every bump in the track I felt in the hard transom. And then they left me with hardly a word at the back of Lige's.

They didn't leave me round the front.

Chapter Three

It was Jas Jonski broke my face could have been my story. Of course it could. I didn't have it in my head though. That's where stories should live. Clear as a nice high stream in the hills. Jas Jonski, a man I had never even kissed. It was all too black to see. This little tempest of shaking kept going through me, head to toe. Someone had forced his way into me too because I was all rags and tatters down there. I could have told them I thought it was him but I don't know what wild horses would have held them back from killing him. It would not matter what John Cole was then, angel or Indian, it wouldn't have stopped him. He'd have gone into town with a fire of vengeance in him and nothing could have saved Jas Jonski.

I didn't want John Cole strung up. And I didn't have the story just right in my head neither.

You only had to look like you done something wrong in America and they would hang you, if you were poor.

Anyway maybe I intended to put the matter right on my own account. I remember having that thought. It was the bravado of my distress. There was a time for your father and mother to fight your battles, I remember thinking, and there was a time to fight them for yourself and I had reached that time I reckoned.

I will say I was very ashamed. I was very ashamed that Rosalee had to clean me. I was in a stupor of shame. I couldn't speak, not even to myself, about that. So in place of speaking I thought – I will settle the matter for myself. Well that was brave enough I guess. Thoughts like that are good for a while, for a moment. But how do you carry them out?

O

It could be I am talking about things that occurred in Henry County, Tennessee in 1873 or 4, but I have never been so faithful on dates. And if they did occur, there was no true account of them at the time. There were bare facts, and a body, and then there were the real events that no one knew. That Jas Jonski was killed was the bare fact. Others were killed too but their killers were known. Who killed him? That was the big question in the town, for a little while. For longer than you might think. Maybe they still talk about it, down there in Paris, Tennessee. If I say that here following are the real events, you will remember that they are described at a great distance from the time of their happening. And that there is no one to agree to or challenge my account, now. Some of it I am inclined to challenge myself, because I say to myself, could that really have happened, and did I really do that? But we only have one path across the mire of remembrance in general.

Beyond the lawyer Briscoe and maybe a few others, in the minds of the townspeople I was not a human creature but a savage. Closer to a wolf than a woman. My mother was killed like a shepherd would kill a wolf. That's a fact too. I guess there were two facts. I was less than the least of them. I was less than the whores in the whorehouse, except maybe for them I was just a whore, in the making. I was less than the black flies that followed everyone in the summer. Less than the old shit thrown to the backs of the houses.

Just something so *less* you could do what you wanted to it, bruise it, hit it, shoot it, skin it.

Just because John Cole raised me up as something so gold, he said, that the sun itself was jealous of me, didn't mean anyone else in the wide world thought that.

❍

The lawyer Briscoe was what Thomas McNulty called an 'original'. When I hear Thomas McNulty's voice in my head, the word is more properly written *riginal*. Lige

Magan said there was no one else like him in all the broad lands of America. Not that anyone knew of.

'A course,' said Lige Magan, 'I ain't met everyone in America.'

The lawyer Briscoe – I never heard him referred to by any other handle – was about sixty years old at the time I got work with him. He still had a head of wiry hair which he kept tamped down with a jar of hair-oil. That hair-oil. It stunk like a rotten cabbage. And the thing I always marvelled at was how clean his hands were. Of course he had no farming to do. But he had little pumice implements that he used for rounding off his nails, and he picked out any bit of dirt with a silver point.

He had been too old to fight in the war but that had probably been a good thing, he said, because like many in Tennessee his head was only dizzy with where to rest his allegiance. His party maybe was life.

He had an office in his house full of glimmering wood so that you might think water was lying just there on the floor, making it shift and tremble. He placed me at a little table in the corner, to do the numbers, beside a window that looked out along the high road. He wanted me to see who was coming and who was going and sometimes he asked me to note down the names, if I knew them. A lot of the people passing were the same people from day to day.

There was Felix Potter the carter for instance, who had his name painted on his cart. If it was a new face I would ask the lawyer Briscoe to hurry to my little window and peer out. I had to make way for his stomach, which stuck out before him. That way I got to know nearly everyone in Paris that had business along the road. Then when someone came to engage him in work, I would usually have some idea who they were, and if there were papers proper to that person already in existence, I would gather them out of the documents cupboard.

Those documents were sometimes speaking things, sometimes silent as snow. There were lists of every black soul bought and sold in Henry County at the Negro Sales Office, which was the lawyer Briscoe's father's work. The monetary history of Mr Hicks's store was there, and four other general stores too, seventy years of provisioning, and years and years of government contracts to supply the vanished Indians — and fifty old sere pages doing the accounts for militias that helped herd the Chickasaw and Cherokee out of Tennessee.

It had proved impossible to civilise us, the documents said. It made me cry to read such things. There was nothing more civilised than my mother's breast, and myself nestled there.

But numbers didn't weep and were needed for everything.

He was very keen that I keep a wary eye on that road. This was so he could stay alive as much as anything else, because strangers at that time in Tennessee after the war were not a trustworthy commodity. And the lawyer Briscoe's views in truth were very East Tennessee for a man that lived in the west of that state. East Tennessee had many that had wanted not to secede. Not only were there oftentimes gaggles of soldiers but also mysterious dark men that might have been soldiers once but had lost at that. Twilight was an awful busy time sometimes on that road. This was even though the new governor was all for the old rebels, and they had got their votes back too, whereas the previous one had been all for the Union, and taking the votes off them – or indeed *because* of that dance of time.

He himself sat at a big table that had come in on the first carts to Tennessee. Nearly a hundred years before, he said, before Tennessee was even Tennessee. His great-grandfather was the first Briscoe in. The lawyer Briscoe had strong feelings about Tennessee. He liked to talk about its old beginnings and he often used an old Tennessee phrase when he was talking, 'between the mountains and the river'. That's where Tennessee lay, according to the lawyer Briscoe, between the Mississippi and the Appalachians. I guess it did lie there. 'Between the two rivers' was a phrase for West Tennessee, because sure enough it lay between the Tennessee river and the Mississippi.

The lawyer Briscoe had what you might call big ideas about the world in general. He was an enthusiast for what he called 'unfashionable causes'. I think I must have been one of them. He thought that the old president Andrew Jackson had done great mischief to the Chickasaw long ago by driving them away to Indian Country. As for Ulysses S. Grant, the present president, he sighed a lot about him. A good soldier maybe but did a good soldier make a good president?

The lawyer Briscoe was married to a woman from Boston and had seven children but his wife had taken the children away with her back to Boston. In her place he had Lana Jane Sugrue to keep house for him, and her two brothers, Joe and Virg, who drove me out to Lige's that time. Lana Jane was from Louisiana and used words like *couture* and *coiffure*. She was very small and wore a hat indoors and out because she was nearly bald.

I sat at my little table and I kept the books. And then at six John Cole would come get me in the cart, because the lawyer Briscoe's house was south of Paris and there was no need so to run the gauntlet of the town. John Cole prompted by the silence of the journey would talk about New England where he was born and all his adventures in the world with Thomas McNulty, which had been many. Sometimes he was gay enough and told me humorous accounts of things but most of the time John Cole was a person that liked to say serious things.

'Most important thing in the world,' he said, 'is anyone who bring harm to you, he likely die.'

The seasons would sit in backdrop to his words and if it was winter he would be buttoned up nearly to the two black sparks of his eyes and myself likewise but somehow he could always keep the talk going, even in the icy days.

When he was around Thomas McNulty, which was as much of the time as he could manoeuvre, he barely said a word.

When Thomas was dressed as my mamma, either way he was just the same. His voice didn't change or anything like that. After he came back from Kansas he didn't put on the dresses so much. If the lawyer Briscoe was a *riginal*, he was one too. Thomas McNulty always said he came from nothing. He meant it to the letter of the phrase. All his people died far away in Ireland, just as mine did in Wyoming. They died of hunger and many Indians died of the same complaint. He said he came from nothing but he lived with kings and queens now. It never entered his head that we were nothing too.

He had this way of jutting out his face when he talked about John Cole, and his chin would go up and down, like the latch on a machine. John Cole was always in

Thomas McNulty's good books. He would blush saying things about him. Just ordinary things, but his cheeks would flush when he said them.

'Guess we gotta ask John Cole about that,' he would say, perhaps, if it was a point of argument. Then his face would jut out. He didn't mean it to be funny but I would laugh. I am sure he saw me laughing but he never paid it any heed. He never asked what was amusing me anyhow. And if he had I couldn't have said.

I could always talk to Thomas McNulty about everything just as easy as you'd like, until I found the limit of that.

◑

Rosalee Bouguereau maybe was sad too when the dress was put aside because it was she who had directed operations as the queen in the shadows and she had gone to the trouble of cutting a hundred bits of white cloth and twisting them about and sewing them as small roses under the neckline. Rosalee Bouguereau had been a true slave till lately as I say but if her mind was on that she didn't show it but only a leaning towards what might best be called happiness.

She wasn't happy the day I came home with bruises. She was mighty distressed as she cleaned me off. She had to go in between my legs. She must have seen a lot of hurt to women when she was a slave.

But of course West Tennessee didn't like black folks either side of the war.

'They don't like no black man getting up,' Lige Magan would say. 'It all just butternut country.'

Lige had the easy-going humour of the victorious soldier that has noticed the perils of victory.

'East Tennessee,' he said, 'was all Lincoln country in the war, they fought in Union blue, just like us – but this West Tennessee – cotton fields and Confederate jackets.' He was shaking his head at this bit of history, as if a thing confounding and confusing, which it was.

'I guess Grant he ain't so bad,' said Thomas McNulty. 'No friend to no butternuts.'

Rosalee Bouguereau couldn't give two hoots about Ulysses S. Grant and the way things turned out maybe she was right in that. She just wanted her pies to come out as she had willed them to do and for us to be at our ease in the winter evenings when weather kept all dreams indoors, and she wouldn't have chosen to be cleaning up after what happened to me, I would wager good money on that.

Her brother Tennyson was trying to work a field for himself and otherwise work for Lige and Lige gave Rosalee a wage for her work in the house and so Rosalee reckoned she had dominion over herself. Just about.

I can't report all these years later that she was welcome in Paris no more than John Cole or myself and she had to keep her eyes to the ground when she walked there. But she did walk there and went into the haberdashery by the back as careful as you like. She knew her ribbons better than old Ma Cohen the haberdasher's wife, I would say that.

She cleaned me that day with the very grace and gentle murmur of a mother.

For a woman who had never been married she knew more about marriage than Thomas McNulty in various particulars. I knew nothing about it in any particular. I guess a whiteman's pastor could have prepared a girl for marriage though I would doubt if such instruction could have been given to me since they wouldn't allow me schooling when I was a little girl. Anyway it mattered not a whit because Rosalee had tried to see to all that. She explained to me how the engines of love would work and what went where and how to brook all that and she explained what men probably liked and what they probably didn't like. This was at the very limit of her knowledge, I'll be bound. She had no model for her wisdom only being a woman herself and in her early years as I say she had lived in the old slave shacks that were still northwest of the great infield in Lige's place, falling back into the weeds and weather. There used to be three dozen slaves. In there, she said, humanity was a book without a cover.

She had got a little enamel basin with hot water in it and a clean rag and she dabbed away at me. Oh mercy. She knew well what had happened but we didn't either of us have words for it, as I recall. The language she employed was gentleness and she cleaned me off and then she put her two arms around me and rocked me and said I was such a good girl and wasn't to mind. But I did mind, terribly, of course. As well she knew. Rosalee's eyes had that queer half-yellow half-orange colour of a harvest moon, I never did see the likes of those eyes again on anyone. She was a kind woman that had been treated like she was nothing for a long time. Lige had a big theory that she was a queen. He liked to say that.

'Who knows but that she might be a queen,' he'd say.

Up to this point, Jas Jonski had been going to be marrying a happy girl. Although Lige's farm, according to Lige, wasn't worth two cents after the war, it gave us enough for immediate needs. And I was in good work. And these had been good days for John Cole and Thomas McNulty too because it was after the great emergency that had befallen Thomas at Fort Leavenworth when his old captain Major Neale swung to his rescue and saved him from the gallows.

I remember well the day he came home after his long time in prison and I don't believe in all the history of the world there was ever so happy a face atop a body as Thomas McNulty's face that day. He had walked down on his own the five hundred miles from Kansas.

For our part John Cole and myself had walked half the road to the town because we knew Thomas McNulty would swing right of the woods and avoid Paris and reappear like a very buck at the trees' edge.

I don't know if you ever saw a man take another man in his arms but if you haven't I can tell you it is a touching sight. Because men are fixed to be so cold and brave, in their eyes. Maybe that afflicted Jas Jonski, but not my two men. They took a grip of each other by the ragged trees and maybe Thomas McNulty was clothed worse than any forest weed, and John Cole to a stranger's eyes was as rough as a ditch, but I knew the story of them in particular and so I could justly suspect the fierce force that burned through them, from one breast to another, in the fever of that embrace.

I suppose if I had had an ambition for Jas Jonski it would have been that he loved me as well as that.

Then Rosalee holding me in her arms.

I guess the world can be sad enough.

Chapter Four

We heard of people hungering elsewhere. The whole south had been burned in the last year of the war and it was sometimes said only weeds could flourish after that. And then the whole wide world went to hell. No money in the banks. What else were banks for but to have money in them? And the *Paris Invigilator* spoke of counties where great crowds of freedmen walked blindly about and ravishments and murders itemised and no one seemed to know when the good turn in things might come. We'd had a president called Andrew Johnson who had been all for saying he was poor dead Lincoln's emissary on earth but really he loved those old beaten rebs. That's what Thomas said. And those beaten rebs were rising, rising all the time.

It wasn't my first time finding the world all flood and fire or my first time to enjoy good days either. Or for outside things to break against a happiness. My own mother when I was a very little girl worked to heap me always with happiness. It was a blessed thing to be a child among my people. The grown women kept the camp and the men hunted and fought and it was our small task as children just to bob about and be happy. That much I remembered clearly enough. We ran about between the teepees and there was nothing to fence us only maybe the temper of an ill-tempered dog. In the winters the foul storms kept us spancelled in our tiny spaces but what was that to us? And we got the long strips of dried meat and snow was melted on the fire. And in the deepest section of the year our teepee must have been like a secret cone inside the big snow, only the wisp of smoke traipsing on the surface to betray where we crouched. My mother's head held good stories and she told them to us as we leaned into her legs for warmth. We had our own language in those times and I can still feel her voice murmuring, her breath a little tempest on my face as I looked up at her. Her arms rested along our backs like fallen branches forgotten there and she uttered her stories. Of wonders and strange times. By being able to make each moment in a child's measure good she made us feel the possible long country of eternity. Many's a time I wept against her knees because I was so happy.

My mother had the fame of great bravery among our tribe. One time when all the men were away a band of Crow who were our enemies came roaming near our village. It was just the women and the children and the old ones. Those Crow were going to take what they could and kill us or whatever they wanted to do. My mother broke from our little group and walked out to the edge of the ground where the Crow were gathered. She greeted them in a friendly way and started to talk to them and soon they were talking pleasantly and so somehow by the magic of her courage that moment of disaster was turned away. People talked about that moment as a sacred thing and she was held in great reverence because of it. Three or four times she was asked to ride with the men to war because they believed she had a special power. They put a man's clothes on her and off she rode. She had this way of knowing where the enemy was in a landscape even when they were hiding. There wasn't a man on this earth could have snuck up on her. Many said to me there was no one ever like her. In that way she was a story herself.

Another story she told was one she called The Fall. A great sickness had come to us, she said, a thousand moons ago. Almost everyone died. They fell down and just hours later were dead. Oh, how we feared that story. A thousand moons ago was her deepest measure of time. It was the same measure as Thomas McNulty's 'a hundred years'. A wandering preacher asked him one time, 'When didst thou come to America, Thomas?' 'A hundred years ago,' was his answer. For my mother time was a kind of a hoop or a circle, not a long string. If you walked far enough, she said, you could find the people still living who had lived in the long ago. 'A thousand moons all at once', she called it. You could not walk so far, she said, but that didn't mean they weren't there. She had all sorts of notions that pleased us greatly as children, and frightened us too.

But the soldiers killed her of course and they killed my father and my uncles. They killed my sister, my aunts, they killed a lot of people. They must have done, because everyone was gone. It was just me then, it felt like.

We were nothing to them. I think now of the great value we put on what we were and I wonder what does it mean when another people judge you to be worth so little you were only to be killed? How our pride in everything was crushed so small it disappeared until it was just specks of things floating away on the wind. Where was my mother's courage then? Was it dust too? We thought the world was called Turtle Island but it turned out it was not. What does that do to your heart, what did it do to mine?

Nothing, nothing, nothing, we were nothing. I think about that and think it is the very rooftop of sadness.

But maybe that was why Thomas McNulty and John Cole loved me, because I was the child of nothing.

Only a few of us little children seemed to escape the massacre to be extracted like thorns from that life and put suddenly into another. Then Mrs Neale taught me my English in the fort and then she gave me to Thomas McNulty when he asked for me. Mrs Neale asked me would I go. And even if I was a little lost girl, and he was a rough soldier, I liked him. I remember sitting there all tidy and small in front of Mrs Neale, making the decision. Yes. They were just going to bring me along as a servant. Maybe she would have given me to them no matter what I said. But I don't know because I said yes. Mrs Neale had a liking for Thomas and she trusted him. I can see now that lots of Indian girls were taken for wicked purposes. That crazy man Starling Carlton, why, it was well known that he was a thief of children, and would bring children off the wild country to people for reasons that were so dark no season of the year and no night of storm could match them.

No, I think it is true I couldn't remember the slaughter. I truly don't think I could.

Now here was a second thing I couldn't remember and it had just happened to me.

In the midst of this Jas Jonski appeared after a couple of weeks. He came clattering up the track on an old horse he must have begged off his friend Frank Parkman at the town livery. Of course I had not been near the town ever since and I suppose he might have been waiting for me to reappear there. Who knows how his mind was working.

It was a late spring day of narrow sunshine with plenty of cold still in it. My trembling had stopped to the naked eye but the very sight of him atop that sorry horse, his red face swaying about, didn't do me good. I wasn't agog to see him again anyhow. Far from it. I stood in the shadows of the parlour and watched him approach, digging his spurs into the sides of the grey mare. The men had been out since five but only as far as the tobacco barn because they were doing work there so they were only a hundred yards off the house.

Rosalee was cleaning Tennyson's rifle and the gun was lying in sections on the kitchen table and there was a thick smell of oil in the room.

'Who coming up the track?' she said, though she hadn't even looked up. I guess she heard the ruckus of the hooves. As I say every stranger was a fear in prospect.

'It that boy Jas Jonski,' I said.

Rosalee abandoned her brother's gun and went to the window, peering out. She looked out fiercely then looked back at the dismantled gun as if she would have liked to have the use of it.

'You wanting to see him?' she said.

'Not so much.'

'You tell him yet about that wedding?'

'I ain't said a word about nothing to him.'

'You want me to tell him he must come another day?'

'I want you to tell him never come.'

As she passed me then she laid a hand on my back in kindness and then went forth into the chill light of the morning. She stomped down the steps and now Jas Jonski was maybe forty feet from her, and I could see him struggling to tie his mare's reins to the stump-post. But that mare was a devil for tossing her head. Rosalee was able to get all the way to him before speaking.

Rosalee was a big woman and it looked like there were two of her to Jas Jonski's skinny one. I could see him smiling his smile, and laughing his little tin laugh, and I saw him lay a hand on her back just as she had done to me. He somehow indicated ownership with his careless touch. But unlike me, Rosalee made a firm step back and she widened her arms and I don't know what she said but I saw Jas Jonski pout his lips and was looking at her like she peed on his shoe. If she wasn't a slave any more to him she was still a lowly person. Then despite his small size he pushed her out of his way imperiously and started towards the house. Me and the house.

Well I retreated back through the parlour and out into the yard there that fell away from the back wall and I ran through the winter-raddled weeds swift as my fear emboldened me and nearly tore off the latch of the wicket gate in the great door of the barn. Lige Magan was a few feet in and he had the huge rake and was raking tobacco dust and the general dust that gathers everywhere on this earth, and I could see Thomas McNulty and John Cole on the upper reach of the tobacco houses, caulking chinks with mud and mortar out of heavy buckets. Lige would burn all that dust against the bad mould and little mushrooms that lurked in a taken harvest. I didn't see Tennyson Bouguereau. No, I saw him, he was sharpening the harrows in a far corner. All late winter they had ploughed the frozen earth till the plough blades screamed. Soon it would be the turn of the harrows.

I was damp now in my dress and I was shaking and I ran across the floor and up the big ladders to John Cole like I was still a little girl and I wrapped myself round him. So much for seeing to things myself. His hands and lap and arms were caked in mud. He printed himself on me. The ten mules stooked in there under the ladders against the cold shivered on their ties and stepped back a few steps on the hard ground.

John Cole begged of me what was amiss and I told him that Jas Jonski was at the house.

'You need to drive him off,' I said.

'Why's that now?' said John Cole.

I said I didn't know exactly but that I would be mighty obliged to him if he would go out and say as much to Jas Jonski and also would he say to Jas Jonski not to bother about coming again.

Thomas McNulty was covered in mud head to foot and when he came over he banged his two hands on his breast and banged his two legs and banged his backside just to urge it off but he didn't get far with that and then he looked at me.

'I'll go out and talk to him,' he said, his voice as grim as I ever heard.

'You do, Thomas,' said John Cole.

Now Lige Magan had made his way up the ladders after me. Lige's father put Rosalee side by side with his own son at school. Only in old slave times could that have happened. That was long years ago. Maybe Rosalee was the only black woman in Tennessee knew Greek, Latin, and Hebrew. Tennyson her brother could neither read nor write so her skills were rare skills. The point is, I never did see even Lige Magan reading a book in the time I knew him but he must have got some of the wisdom Rosalee got. Anyway he stayed Thomas McNulty from going.

'I think best thing is I go down and bring his orders,' he said.

He meant bring orders to Jas Jonski. The world was all army to Lige.

When I think about it, we were poised for danger there in Henry County, with three men that had fought for the Union, except, that was the point. They were soldiers through and through. Tach Petrie found he couldn't budge them, and he had five, six men to command, they being hardened men that used to wear the light blue jacket.

Lige Magan went down into the dusty bowel of the barn again and plucked up his rifle. With a little hasty glance up at us he pushed on through the wicket and the wicket banged and the darkness came back into the barn. Our faces were turned towards where we *imagined* Lige Magan was crossing the yards to Jas Jonski.

A minute, two minutes passed. Had we even breathed out? Then there was a great bang and Thomas McNulty looked startled and he looked at John Cole and then tried to make a decision to stay or go and then he must have thought he'd better go in case that Jas Jonski had got a gun after all – and he hurried away.

Then there was silence for a long time. Not a sound came up to tell us anything.

Chapter Five

'So he the one that did it?' said Lige Magan.

We were in the cabin at that familiar table. Rosalee Bouguereau sat at my side, and Thomas McNulty the other. Thomas McNulty had his arms crossed and was gazing at me, nodding his greybeard face. John Cole was standing at the window but if he was looking out the queer blind stare in his eyes denied it. Tennyson Bouguereau wasn't there, he was in the linen room yonder with Jas Jonski.

'He didn't say that,' said Thomas McNulty. 'He said it weren't him. He said why in the name of tarnation would he come out if it was him who done it. That's what he said, just now. Even when you put your rifle under his chin, Lige, he swore it weren't him.'

'Then I guess we have to beat him till he tells the truth,' said Lige Magan, just flaring up. 'He looked guilty to me. Why, he was all fixed to make a run when he saw me come out. Was going to run like the guilty right enough. When I fire that shot he stopped like a statue. Then he's looking back, all white face. Then you come, Thomas, and then I ask him that question, and he don't say nothing, and the piss running down his trews, and then I ask again, with the help of the gun, and right enough he say he didn't do nothing. He says he never even knew nothing had happen. Waited ten days to hear from Winona and not a word. His *fiancée* he called her. Came out just to see what was what.'

Lige Magan looked at Thomas McNulty with that particular look that meant, Well, what you say to that?

But Thomas McNulty didn't answer. He put a hand on my sweating back. I was crying like a spring rain. I was shaking. Shaking again. I felt sick as a poisoned person. Thomas McNulty was paying heed to that talk of mine, that strange talk with no words that was pouring out of me. I never felt so sad, sick, and scared. Even when I was trying to get home with Lana Jane Sugrue's brothers. I didn't know what was wrong with me, not to itemise. I didn't want to hear any more talk. I wanted everything to go back to where it was before, me and the white dress, and working for the lawyer Briscoe, and thinking about kissing Jas Jonski.

'Well, we got to know what to do,' said Lige Magan, the anger gone out of him as quick as it came in. 'Can't leave him tied up in the linen room if he ain't done nothing, goddamn it.'

'We spring him if we believe him,' said John Cole

firmly. 'I don't know if I care to believe him. He just a skunk.'

'You care if Sheriff Flynn come out here with twenty deputies and knock everything along to hell,' said Lige Magan. 'We just got to know what happened.'

He was looking at me then. I was seeing him through the cascade of tears. I didn't know what Rosalee Bouguereau had said to them even. About the torn parts. All that. I never even kissed that boy. Did he tear me like that? Was it him that did that? I was screaming at myself inside of myself, screaming with my mouth open so loud. Not that they saw that. But Thomas McNulty was a wise old person, he could feel things happening to other folk, I think he could.

'See, if you don't remember nothing,' said Thomas, to Lige Magan, 'it don't mean it don't done happen, that's a fact.'

'I going to put my girl into her bed and I going to give her my rabbit soup,' said Rosalee Bouguereau, angrily too, scraping back her chair and standing up. 'Look at this girl. She can't even sit.'

I could feel myself melting away. I thought I was like water but I had no cup to hold me. How small I felt. World didn't care, I knew that. The world outside what we were at Lige's place. World wanted bad things to happen to Indian girls. That was what I was thinking, when

I was thinking. Mostly I was trying to hold up my melting head. Hold my melting arms, my melting legs. I was just a girl, wasn't I? I was so glad for Rosalee being there, a kind woman like that.

But they were all kind. It was just they didn't know what to do and they had known a thousand times what to do in bad times. That was why they were still alive and I was still alive. I was still alive and now I feared I was dead somehow. I thought someone had killed me right enough. How was I ever going to rise again? How would I get my limbs back? How would I be happy again, foolish happy as you need to be in this life? Stand on the porch of a spring morning and feel the cold in the sunlight but also the rumour of summer? What a foolish little child I had been – but that was the best sort of character to hold, in all the history of the world. A foolish little child loved by all who knew her unless it was an ignorant farmboy seeing just only an Indian's black hair in the town. Maybe it was a foolish farmboy that hurt me, maybe it was. I was peering and peering back now, trying to bursting to see that. Oh, if it wasn't Jas Jonski maybe there was a hope for me in that.

'I ain't saying it was Jas,' I said.

Then I was not there. So Rosalee told me. I fainted back onto the floor and Thomas McNulty scooped me up and then Rosalee said I was carried to my bed – the deep warm bed I shared with her – and I was told that Lige Magan took that as gospel and went into the linen room and let Jas Jonski loose. Jas Jonski went and got his shaky horse and fled away.

◑

The lawyer Briscoe turned up a while later. Joe Sugrue brought him out in the buggy.

That was the best buggy in Henry County. My guess was he had needed that for his grand wife and now all he had was the grand buggy that used to carry her grandness.

Well I just plumb cried when I saw him coming in because that was the state I was in.

He came in the door like a spoon is put into a bowl of grits. The dark room took the gleams off his face. Rosalee Bouguereau battered the coffee pot on the stove with unusual clumsiness. She was excited to see such an important man.

He was content to sit in an old oak chair that Lige Magan supplied for him, near the stove. Because the hoarfrost had been raging all night along the sere meadow grasses. He kept on his fur hat and his fur coat all the same. He spoke for a little about the weather and asked Lige Magan how the planting was going and he commented on the parlous state of everything in Henry County and Lord would it ever find its feet again and then having given its due to convention he said what he had come to say. He said he had heard disturbing news about his employee as he called me and thought he was obliged and obligated moreover to come out and have a look-see what had occurred.

'Well,' said Lige Magan, 'you see she got a big fright and no mistake.'

'I heard. Joe Sugrue told me and I was very annoyed to hear it,' he said. 'But those numbers won't tally theyselves and I would be obliged if Winona could come back to me *instanter*.'

I was standing a bit caught-out centre floor and I was making all the effort that was in me to comport myself. You can't be a geyser of tears all your life.

'She got to have some recompense in law,' said Lige Magan.

'An Indian ain't a citizen and the law don't apply in the same way,' said the lawyer Briscoe.

'Is that what you say?' said John Cole, very quietly, but with a nice dash of menace in it.

The men were looking at each other and taking that in, I suppose, and John Cole was looking like he might go on fire any moment soon as a next step after the menace.

'Now is the time for being peaceful and living quietly.

You are old men, just like me,' the lawyer Briscoe said. 'What the hell age *are* you, Lige, does even God know?'

'I don't believe He does,' said Lige, inclined to lift towards laughter, but stopping it best he could.

John Cole, who was somewhat in the shadow of this encounter, shifted on his boots – very like a horse that feels the need to shift his weight in the byre.

'I ain't but forty years old,' said Thomas McNulty, though in truth he didn't know what age he was exactly. 'And I believe some wicked person . . .' he went on, and then floundered.

'You believe what?' said the lawyer Briscoe sharply.

'I believe some wicked person got to be brought to account for what he done to Winona,' Thomas said, 'since you asking' – suddenly finding the words.

'I believe that too,' said Rosalee Bouguereau. The lawyer Briscoe stared at her a moment. Was he surprised? No. Just then Rosalee had finally gotten the coffee to her satisfaction and had brought it with a cup hooked on her finger to him.

'I say we find out who did the deed and go and shoot that man,' said John Cole.

Thomas McNulty and Rosalee looked in agreement. Thomas McNulty opened his hands as if to say, how about that, Mr Briscoe?

'Ain't anyone else drinking coffee?' the lawyer Briscoe

said. No one answered and he allowed Rosalee to fill his cup.

'You got molasses?' he asked her, quietly, like he was suddenly in another place with her, like we weren't there just then.

'Ain't you got some of that New Orleans molasses?' said Lige Magan to Thomas McNulty, anxious despite everything to give his visitor what he craved.

'I poured it away,' said Thomas McNulty roughly.

'You like cane sugar, Judge?' Rosalee said.

'I do, I do,' said the lawyer Briscoe. 'And I thank you, Miss Bouguereau. I ain't no judge by the by.'

Then Rosalee fetched the sugar and tipped a little in and the lawyer Briscoe drank his coffee.

While he was drinking he didn't speak. Nor did anyone else. Each in our different brains turning around what had been said and what had not been said.

I didn't know what I needed to hear. When a flood goes through a farm there's so many trees down and then the crops themselves if they are up are pressed down too. The worst flood will be the whole kingdom of every last field needing to be ploughed over all again and then harrowed afresh and maybe you are too late in the year to get in another sowing just that year. So maybe in the aftertime of that flood and after you have dried out your clothes you will see that you will not eat next year just as good as you did this year. But what is plain as your face is that you have to meet the great force of the flood, or the tornado, or the great storm, with an equal great force. To build up what has been torn down and to put back in their places what has been rended from their places and parted from their hooks.

The lawyer Briscoe went on quietly with his coffee drinking.

Chapter Six

I need to say a few things about Tennyson Bouguereau. Since it was that they beat him. It was to do with it being him that held Jas Jonski captive a little while. That's what was said later, a black man holding sway over a white man. That's what those ignorant people called uppity. There were many folks in Henry County couldn't hear that and not want to punish him. They knew how to do it.

I was sure Jas Jonski wasn't afraid to proclaim his innocence in the town. He was part of that crowd of young men his age who went blazing about. Blazing about and yammering nonsense.

I remember in the old days on the plains how all the young Lakota boys went about together too. I suppose young white folks are the same. A girl is a more solitary thing. Even so I remember the three days spent dancing when a girl got finally her 'moon'. I don't remember the Lakota word but it meant moon. I remember the singing and dancing and there was great pride in the young women. When I got my moon first, I think I was twelve or so, I wasn't with my people, I was up with the poet McSweny in Grand Rapids, while Thomas McNulty and John Cole were away at the war. The poet McSweny was a black person like Rosalee and he was a famous doorman at the theatre up there but when I got my moon I thought I was going to die and he did too. He was about ninety years old at the time so he might have known better. But we were two ignorant creatures there in that house of his. He went running for Doc Ganley that lived some doors along and the doc came running back with him and when he saw how it was with me, he laughed. The poet McSweny was instructed in this aspect of the world and was obliged to cut one of his old bedsheets into bandages for me. That's how that went along. There was no dancing or singing or women that knew what to do.

Jas Jonski was young like all the young that ever lived, white or black or red. I didn't know at that time if it was him that saw Tennyson Bouguereau when he was in town. I supposed it might have been. Our wagon was found half heeled into the woods and poor Jakes our best mare shaking and sad in the harness. As I remember it was not so far from the lawyer Briscoe's house, so some men led the horse and wagon down there and I think they thought they had done their duty then. They hadn't even paid any heed to the unconscious body of the poor black man strewn right there on the road.

If you wanted to have a picture of sorrow a travelling photographer might have taken a daguerreotype of Rosalee Bouguereau's face when that news came. I rushed to her and drew her into an embrace. She wept and wept.

'It's alright, Rosalee, hush now,' Lige Magan said, 'least he ain't dead.'

That night John Cole and Lige Magan came back with her brother. They had ridden off on mules after hearing the bad news from the Sugrue brothers and now they came back with the same mules hitched to the back of the wagon and the big tin lamp pouring its light onto everything. Jakes the mare was still trembling. A horse is a knowing person. And Tennyson Bouguereau's poor broken body lying in the bed of the wagon. His handsome face swollen with bruises and blood and his clothes that he always kept so neat like the raiment of a beggar-man.

So that's why I wanted to say things about Tennyson. Tennyson Bouguereau was famous, among us at least, for his skill with a rifle. Lige Magan said many times about how Tennyson set up a blade of grass one time and walking back fifty feet then turned with his Spencer and shot the blade of grass into two pieces. Lige Magan was in a position to appreciate that skill because he himself had been a sharpshooter in the army but never as sharp as Tennyson. Tennyson Bouguereau had a natural God's ability to do it. Of course as a former slave he could only bear arms in great privacy. Just for a while everything had been looking better for those slaves. They had downed tools on farms they didn't like to work on any more. They had got the vote, well, the men had. They could look a whiteman in the eye and talk to him straight as an arrow. Just for a while. Now it was heaving back the other way. Farmers thereabouts had no one to work their farms if the black workers wouldn't stay. Everyone was getting crazy about it. Big bursts of violence would be told of, and evil things done and said. The fact was, Tennyson Bouguereau was quite the prince of a man. He would have helped anyone if anyone asked or was in need of his help.

He couldn't read or write but he could draw your face on Rosalee's nice paper and he liked to draw robins in the yard and the only reason I knew what the sleep-all-day whippoorwill looked like was because Tennyson had captured one – on that paper.

The men who beat him didn't care much about all that. Whitemen in the main just see slaves and Indians. They don't see the single souls. How all are emperors to those that love them.

We had to eat scraps for our victuals that evening. Rosalee cleaned her brother off of all stains and she had Lige Magan help her put him to heal into the narrow bedroom at the back where Tennyson slept. I saw her fix his hair with some pomade that John Cole possessed. Tennyson didn't have a single word to say. He was robbed of all his words. She begged him to say who had done the deed but he just stared back like an affrighted child. I saw a long bruise as dark as land just ploughed that was darkening even worse where some implement had hammered at his skull. She got me to crush up the flower-heads of hyacinth that she had gathered and dried in the spring of the previous year and that she always gave to me when I had my moon and she put some of that in the water that she washed him with, so he smelled then a bit like spring. She was trying to wash the violence off of him.

◑

Now Rosalee was the sad one and I was the soup maker. My care for Rosalee was a little charm to me. A human person finds a little medicine in another's sadness. So I found. But it's not so strange because the world is mysterious anyhow.

She was confounded to see her brother so ill-treated. It brought back all the terror of older times to both of them when they never knew if they were to be sunk in servitude forever or free. There were bitter truths to taste despite all, that was for certain.

I come from the saddest story that ever was on the earth. I'm one of the last to know what was taken from me and what was there before it was taken. That's a weight of sadness has crushed many a head. Ever seen a drunken Indian, ever seen an Indian in rags? That's what happens when a king is heaped with sadness. It isn't just that though. We thought it was all riches and wonders what we were. We knew it was. Just how it was possible to be so happy as a child. A world that has made itself good for a child is a good world. It wasn't just that that world was removed. But that the order was so often given, *Kill Them All*. Ask Thomas McNulty, he heard it plenty. He went and obeyed it. John Cole too. That wild boy Starling Carlton. Why, Lige Magan. Didn't matter if it was a baby or a girl or a mother.

Just the touch of a whiteman, just the very approach, was the herald of death.

We set a great value on each living one of us. But the white people's value set on us was not the same measure. We were nothing so to kill us all was just the killing of nothing so it meant nothing. It wasn't a crime to kill an Indian because an Indian wasn't anything in particular.

I know these things so I am writing them down.

◐

Tennyson Bouguereau was a sort of a citizen now so maybe someone beating him was a crime. Didn't they fight that whole war about that? You would think so. That was why the poet McSweny told Thomas McNulty and John Cole they best be going fighting. Or maybe just Thomas was looking at the poet McSweny and seeing what a remarkable soul he was. I mean, a king too, and desolate enough, but such a man with a light of gold around his old head. He was like those paintings of Jesus Christ with the gold ring on top. The poet McSweny. Thomas and John Cole were gone a long stretch that time and I needed to be near them. I wasn't cured of life then and maybe I am not now. But then not, for certain. But the poet McSweny with his dark narrow face and his river-stone eyes, he bestirred himself on my account and schooled me and scolded me and did all the work of a mother.

How was I so lucky to have those good-as-women men? Only a woman knows how to live I believe because a man is too hasty, too half-cocked, mostly. That half-cocked gun hurts at random. But in my men I found fierce womanliness living. What a fortune. What a great heap of proper riches.

Now even with Tennyson Bouguereau laid up and maybe more so because of that, the men were out harrowing the earth that was just then loosening to spring.

The mules had been given their strengthening feed and the old black rack of harrows tied to them and off they went acre after acre turning our dark earth. A mule is a happy boy with a belly of oats in him. You'd expect a mule to laugh then he looks so set up.

Of course the only boy who could go into Paris for provisions now was Lige, just for the moment. Handily there were five dry-goods stores in Paris so Mr Hicks lost our business.

'Just can't be looking at that streaky Jas Jonski,' said Lige.

'Because you might kill him,' said John Cole quietly.

I was just out on the porch to fetch in some underclothes I was drying for Rosalee when I caught sight across the rough acre of a horse and rider. I was pierced through with alarm. Rosalee and Tennyson weren't the only ones made jumpy. If ever ducks were sitting it seemed to me we were those ducks.

Whoever this was coming, he wasn't alone. I saw a straggle of other men bumping on their ponies. My own men were two wide fields off northward. If I had climbed the roof I could have seen them, with the black mules in miniature, and their black figures small as weevils. Tennyson's rifle was always in the parlour – apart from the fact it was such a handsome gun someone had etched the name *LUTHER* on the breechblock, a mysterious but distinguishing mark – so I fetched that and then I took up my position again on the porch with the Spencer for an ally. I knew how to fire a rifle well enough even though it's a big gun for a girl.

It was Sheriff Flynn was the front rider. I didn't know if that was good or bad. He wasn't a person I knew in particular. I would see him go by, clacking his boots along the boardwalk in town. And three men with him. Three scraggled-looking sorts. He was riding at the front just as easy as you like. He was in no hurry to reach me. In no hurry in all the world.

Sheriff Flynn finally reached me and astride his horse was on a level with me where I stood on the porch.

'You go in and get Elijah, honey,' he said.

I never in my life heard Lige given his long name. I never in my life was called honey. He didn't even seem to see the Spencer rifle. I was holding it aslant in my left hand but he didn't seem to see it. I wasn't even sure it had bullets in it. I was thinking, maybe it doesn't, because, well, I didn't know. I knew these boys would shoot me as easy as a rabbit would be shot along the margin of the lands. Quick as that. I felt the piss run down my legs under my skirts. I didn't want anyone seeing that. My body was afraid but my heart was high enough. It was anger for Tennyson made me brave and I thought indeed that Tennyson's rifle would have great medicine in it. It was Tennyson's great pride that he owned it and even to touch it gave me courage.

I didn't make any reply to Sheriff Flynn. Because I didn't know to speak or not to speak.

Sheriff Flynn was a rough dark man but his cheeks were shaved around his moustache and he was likely forty years old and I expect the women in town thought he was handsome enough. His deputies were a bag of ratty men. I knew one of them, now seeing them closer. Frank Parkman. He was a bosom pal of Jas Jonski's.

It was surprising to me how much I could be thinking thoughts as I was standing there, not answering Sheriff Flynn.

Sheriff Flynn dismounted and climbed the steps of the cabin and on reaching me on the porch raised his right hand and I think now was going to shake mine. That was so unexpected I thought first he meant to strike me and I jumped back and tripped over the rifle and down I fell. I got to my feet again immediately. You have got to show a bear or a coyote you are not afraid. The rifle went skittering across the boards. I reckoned if I tried to get it he would shoot me. For the purposes of shooting he had a brightly polished pistol in his belt and that meant he was what Thomas McNulty called a *kittoge*.

'Elijah in there?' said Sheriff Flynn.

'She thinks she going to get whupped,' said Frank Parkman, laughing.

'Shut your damn mouth, Parkman,' said Sheriff Flynn. 'Or I'll whup *you*, you damn fool.'

But he didn't go on with that. Because just now Thomas McNulty and John Cole came around the cabin, and around the other side came Lige Magan. They were all three covered in black soil from the harrowing. They were wearing boots of black soil but of course they weren't real boots. They were coming in for their supper after the long long hours of work.

'How do, Elijah?' said Sheriff Flynn.

'How do,' said Lige Magan.

Sheriff Flynn leaned his elbows on the porch rail and was at his ease and it was a signal for his men to sit back in their saddles and Frank Parkman dismounted and hooked the reins in the crook of his arm and started to stuff tobacco in a little clay pipe he had taken from his coat. I didn't know what Thomas and John Cole were thinking but they decided to swing their legs around the old chairs that were always set out there and Lige Magan himself took up a kind of sentry position at the dark door into the house. He shut the door fast with his free hand without looking at what he was doing.

'You putting in tobacco again this year?' said Sheriff Flynn, not truly a question but a statement of fact. He was nodding at the black soil that marked them.

'We is,' said Lige.

'You grow baccy I smoke it,' said Frank Parkman, puffing away now.

'Ain't no market for beets or nothing,' said Lige. 'Thinking about a little corn maybe. I hope to get forty cents a bushel on that. Only God knows if I will. Or anyone.'

The sheriff said nothing for a good long while and Frank Parkman stood there half smiling, sucking on his pipe.

I had such an itch to go for the Spencer rifle where it lay.

'You the boy that was up in Leavenworth,' said Sheriff Flynn, looking over with a measure of friendliness at Thomas McNulty, as if that was a question often asked in the country generally, that he knew something about Thomas McNulty as normal as rain and he was just saying it. Thomas McNulty must have adjudged that the silence he offered this question was the wisest answer to it.

'He got a discharge writ out and everything,' said John Cole.

'I ain't saying he don't,' said Sheriff Flynn.

Frank Parkman burst out laughing, making his pipe bubble with spit.

'You likely surprised to hear I come out to help you

all,' said Sheriff Flynn. 'You likely surprised to hear the lawyer Briscoe come to see me. You likely surprised to hear Mrs Flynn the elder was at schooling with Rosalee Bouguereau and has fond recollection of her.'

'That a lot of surprise,' said John Cole.

'I guess so,' said Sheriff Flynn. 'I like to find out who hurt Tennyson Bouguereau and who hurt Winona Cole. And so I come out here all seven miles in the good sunlight.'

There was another different class of a silence. I was amazed, but frightened too. I wasn't thinking of firing the Spencer now but how could I give answers when I didn't know the true story of anything?

'No one care a curse about an Indian,' said John Cole. He was like a preacher reading the bible. 'Why you come out here? We know how to do something about things. The minute Tennyson he tell who beat him so bad we going to put the saddles on the mules and go kill those men whoeverso done it.'

'I don't like that plan,' said Sheriff Flynn. 'These are troubled times. You need to don the bonnet of Solomon.'

'We like it fine,' said John Cole. 'We ain't got need of badges and lawmen. We do our own work. And then when if and ever Winona can say who hurt her I say we without interval saddle up again and go killing whoeverso was so evil-bent.'

'You ain't out west here,' said Sheriff Flynn. 'This the new world of homesteads and pickled pears and peace, and holding off and sheriffs come with all that.'

'You see,' said John Cole, 'we ain't going along particular with all that. Because no one care a curse about an Indian – or a black man.'

'You do what you say and you boys finished here in Henry County,' said Sheriff Flynn.

'The whole country very troubled is true and I don't know how we to hold on here if we add to it,' said Lige Magan, as if he was trying that Solomon bonnet for size.

'And yet there must be justice in these troubled times and I aim to try and bring that justice to you,' said Sheriff Flynn.

'I don't know why you want to bring . . .' began Frank Parkman, in sudden anger.

'I told you, Parkman, you got to shut up,' said Sheriff Flynn. But Frank Parkman didn't want to.

'That girl ain't nothing,' he said, a strange whine infecting his voice. 'These folks are scum.'

Sheriff Flynn stepped over to him and slapped his face so hard his hat flew off. He was just waiting for Parkman to say another word, one hand on his Colt revolver. But the deputy just rubbed his reddened cheek.

Now there was a queer speaking silence. Even our winter guest the whippoorwill who had been inclined to start his curious song now the first taint of evening was seeping in held off. I knew all my life with them that Thomas McNulty and John Cole were thinking men but their thoughts were always how to go on living. The other thing was Thomas McNulty and John Cole lived and thought as one. If one were to die there would be no more living then. But also their true thoughts were contained in all that they taught me as a daughter. They found folk to esteem me and when there was no esteem they cut out that element like cankers. Sheriff Flynn was a man of forty in a morass of violent hatreds and counted mutilations and all the history of the war and all the history of what war will do even to private souls and then what comes after war. Make them murderous and violent and mutilating just as quick unless there is a heart to temper and a will to love. That was Thomas McNulty, that was so, and John Cole too. Now here was a half-rough half-shaven sheriff saying and doing new startling things.

I was thinking if I'd have had more courage earlier I would have shot him with the Spencer. So that would have been an end to that and we would have never heard that strange talk. The river of things goes on or sometimes takes a swirling turn. Of course, all turns, all shallows and rapids lead eventually to the sea. The story of a life goes only to the same shore. I could have shot Sheriff

Flynn and then I would have had a story struck by a sudden turn.

But, just like the river, later, it all came to the same thing.

Chapter Seven

It scared me to travel the road but I thought I owed the lawyer Briscoe such a debt that it was fitting rightly to box my fear and violation deep inside me. It was the first time I took the grave precaution to wear the 'better' pair of trews that Thomas McNulty lent me. I didn't need to shorten the legs because he wasn't much taller than me. I took in a little jacket of his that was some sort of fatigues from long ago and flattened my bodice with a scrap of sheeting and I had a good cotton blouse that did service for a shirt. I cared not a whit for my long black hair though I did remember it was sorrow alone that made a Lakota person shear their locks so didn't that stand right? John Cole took my hair and wrapped it in paper and laid it in a drawer. I put my lady's pistol in my belt behind and wore my knife in my left boot. I wasn't the only girl in those times to try to cool men's eyes with the appearance of a boy and I had already learned the folly of not doing so. Not that I had much in the way of bosoms. Not like Rosalee, part of whose charm was that soft immensity. I knew of that immensity because we were obliged to share a bed. It was only four foot wide so at night in the great cold that was a blanket over Tennessee we curled up together. Rosalee Bouguereau didn't own much except her warming character but that was a great possession. Otherwise, she had two dresses. She had a box of letter paper that was made in the paper mill along the Tennessee river that Lige had got for her for writing lists. She took great pride in that. Even if she had no one to send a letter to.

And I took no cart but just our fleetest mule. Ready to spur myself to safety if needs be, as I told myself. But shaking in my new apparel, moving between the roadside trees just themselves shaking off winter I felt very alone even with my gun and my knife. That little wind that prefers the woods seemed like the whispers of murderers of many hues.

'Mercy me,' said Lana Jane Sugrue, 'what have you done to your beautiful *coiffure*?' She laughed and gaped and jumped around me eager to see all angles.

I guess I was a fright for the Sugrue boys who didn't even understand me in a dress but the lawyer Briscoe grunted his assent to this appearance and anyhow his first emergency was the numbers piling up and the wilful sheaf of documents needing to be given regimen. Land deeds in disarray and no one to work great lengths of that ruined country with the slaves amazed by freedom and 'farms destroyed by fire and war' still not brought back to good health according to the lawyer Briscoe with anger in his face as much as tears and old soldiers with their lives in tatters just as much by living on as dying and one day rebels down and next day rebels up. What was a loyal man to do? And loyal to what? And no one Tennessee person just as good as he thought he was and no one maybe also just as bad. Tennessee going to be one thing, the best goddamn Union state in the Union and then going to be another thing, with this change of governor. First it was Governor Brownlow all ready to quash bad feeling against the slaves, and then it was a new jackass trying to drag Tennessee back to hatred and hurt. The onetime rebels with the vote again and there'd never be a Republican governor in Tennessee again, reckoned the lawyer Briscoe. Not that he could see, and his eyes were purty good enough.

The lawyer Briscoe's nib scratching on, regardless, catching in the rags of that bad paper that was the only paper to be had those times. The war had killed the paper mill along the river. So bad paper became 'good enough' paper. The work had to be done.

◐

There was no getting a word, fancy or otherwise, out of Tennyson Bouguereau. He was just as friendly and easy as always but there was something in the engine of himself not working. He hadn't stayed in his bed a moment longer than he had to and he was moving about the barns and the yards as he always did, and could do his work just as Lige instructed. He had been a man that knew a hundred songs but they had fallen silent in him. I could see him strain to make a sound but there wasn't a sound at his command. The raw wound in his hair healed but something deeper stayed awry.

◐

It was good to be at the lawyer Briscoe's in the sense that that was where you would get the news. Sheriff Flynn had gone to the officer in command of the soldiers in Paris and he had told Sheriff Flynn to speak to the colonel of the militia. This was in respect of the battery of Tennyson, not my poor self.

The lawyer Briscoe was very interested in the militia because they had been set in by the former governor of Tennessee himself to do something about the rabblement of rebels and nightriders causing mayhem everywhere. Now it wasn't certain who the militia was supposed to protect or what it was supposed to do. Colonel Purton was the commander and he was fierce against nightriders and all lawbreakers certainly. Henry County was all old rebel country so there was no shortage of them. The thought of a black man rising up to freedom heated their brains the worst of all. So the lawyer Briscoe reckoned that was what had happened to Tennyson. A Negro was supposed to carry a certificate of work and if he didn't he could be considered to be a vagrant. And Tennyson was driving a nice wagon with a lovely mare. So that could be called stealing. Why not? You could say any damn thing about a Negro. So the lawyer Briscoe reckoned that was what had happened. He didn't rightly know. And he didn't rightly know whether the men who did that had any connection to Jas Jonski, but he devised a good method to find out – he thought he would just go and ask Jas.

That's when Jas Jonski as it happened spoke freely enough. He said he was sorry to hear about Tennyson Bouguereau but at the same time he hadn't been shy to say what happened out at that damn farm of Lige Magan's. He was offended and he said Tennyson Bouguereau had treated him insultingly. A man that was a slave only ten harvests back. I said to the lawyer Briscoe that I didn't imagine Tennyson could have done anything but keep his bonds tight and not let him wiggle free, since that was what Lige Magan had told him to do. Well, Jas Jonski said he hadn't been shy about telling his story to anyone would listen. So people heard of this insult to him and how put out he had been and he was only trying to visit his fiancée. So the lawyer Briscoe concluded that the message had got out to those dark folk called nightriders that the militia were meant to chastise. It was considered that the nightriders would soon be coming in now the climate had warmed towards them. Maybe some of those renegade types liked it out in the woods. Better than being married to their dull wives, opined the lawyer Briscoe. He asked if Jas Jonski had pointed Tennyson out to anyone when Tennyson was in the town and Jas Jonski laughed. That laughter was better evidence than words.

So the lawyer Briscoe felt he was making progress and the thing for him was he knew the country was in hardship and disarray but he thought maybe his beloved country of Tennessee might come good out of the war and the consequences of war otherwise known as peace if it only kept an eye on justice.

'The time is so dangerous that the law is barely possible.'

That's what he said. Now he could be said to be glowing a bit when he did, and his red face seemed to swell up a bit in the shadows of the office. That part of the lawyer Briscoe that was of Tennessee was subject to sudden tears. I wasn't feeling weepy when he spoke, I was feeling wretched. Every time he said the name Jas Jonski my heart shrank and my legs were weak. I thought of the hurt between my legs and I wanted to ask the lawyer

Briscoe where my justice was going to come from. My difficulty was I didn't know how much Rosalee had said to the men and I found I hadn't the words to speak of it for myself. I might have said it the very first day I staggered back but all this time between had hardened the words into a stony clump and I was as short for words on that as Tennyson was on everything. I didn't know if Jas Jonski was on the lawyer Briscoe's mind just because of the clash with Tennyson or whether the lawyer Briscoe's thoughts also extended back to Jas Jonski coming out in the first place and my confusion, my confusion over the matter. Goddamn it, as Thomas would say. Goddamn confusion and I even wanted to go back to the moments of my suffering just to see, just to see, who was there causing it. Dark, dark, dark, dark.

My clue was the darkness and my best thought was whoever was the author of the deed must have done the deed in a dark place. I wondered again and again was it the stables where Frank Parkman worked, I didn't know why my mind kept going there. Was it that strange whiny voice he had, maybe? A memory stirred by that? Only, did I remember Jas Jonski bringing me there, or was that just a thought because of the fact that Frank Parkman was a deputy for Sheriff Flynn and so had ridden out to us, all accidentally? I did seem to see in my inner eye myself and Jas Jonski wandering along Court

Square together, arm in arm. Was that mocking words I heard from a little woman outside the Negro Sales building, and was that Frank Parkman standing in the jaws of the stable door and laughing? Laughter again better evidence than words? I was seeing these things and then not seeing them. Passing in and out of sight like in a dream.

◐

How common it is to have your memory of things all muddied up I don't know. It sure played the devil with me.

I was of course reluctant to tell the lawyer Briscoe that myself and Jas Jonski had been drinking whiskey at the back of the store on the fateful day. He had borrowed a bottle from Mr Hicks's stock. He was growing restless under Mr Hicks's yoke, he said, and it pleased him to sequester things that would go unnoticed. A river of whiskey went through the store. I had never had whiskey before and it burned my mouth and I didn't like it much. John Cole was against whiskey in general even though Lige Magan kept a jug of some fiery stuff made in the west of Henry County over near Como. Lige Magan's motto was, two glasses heaven, three glasses hell.

This was no firewater Jas Jonski offered me. It was proper distillery whiskey. I can't remember how much I swigged but if at first I didn't like it much a few minutes later I thought I was a long flower and out of my head was rising and widening a wondrous bloom. I thought I was an angel tempered hard by fire. All my story so far was briefly crossed out and in its place was a strange flame of ecstasy. When I walked out into Paris with Jas Jonski I was floating on burning wings.

The next clear memory is Lana Jane Sugrue shouting for her brothers to hitch the buggy.

So what was I supposed to say happened between? I couldn't be making up a story. There was no purpose in that. It did occur to me that I might take my courage in my hands and sneak into town and ask Frank Parkman what he knew. With his lopsided smile and his laughter, and his whine. From how Sheriff Flynn had dealt with him I knew that the good sheriff thought he was a fool. But I wasn't so sure. There was something there, an echo, a shadow, that was bothering me. And even a fool can harbour a story.

So I went into town that very Friday, after my work with the lawyer Briscoe. I let the mule scuff about the last stretch of the Huntingdon road, walking up and down for an hour, so that the darkness could claim the fringes of the town. A stableboy couldn't leave his stables. I felt pretty sure I would find Frank Parkman in his place of work.

Of course I was in my boy's clothes and I was going to have to see if he recognised me or not as Winona. I reckoned it would be best if he didn't, but then, he might be surprised to find there was yet another damn Indian in Paris. When you haven't spun out much of a plan of what to say you can begin to feel pretty stupid as you approach your task. Would he accept me as a cousin of Winona, if I said so? Would he just laugh his crazy boy's laugh at me, and see instantly who it was? Then as a friend of Jas Jonski would he not just clam up? I only wanted to get a clear view of the truth. That was all I was out to gain. After all, he was a deputy of the law now and then, clearly enough, and wasn't it his clear duty to bolster the truth, especially as his boss Sheriff Flynn had come out to Lige's saying he was fixed to find out things?

The town in twilight was like one of those kettles of food starting to boil. Invisible people were lighting candles and lamps in the houses just now being rubbed out slowly by nightfall. All the colours of the place not especially gay in the first instance were now darkening brown plank by plank. The only house with a bit of sparkle and fuss was Zollicoffer's saloon and the sound of the piano there was running out into the streets and private spaces of the town like a hundred rats. My mule was a creature of good grace and despite being a lowly breed enough had a fine step to his gait, there was something of those little Mexican horses about him. He had no need to be ashamed of himself anyhow. With the lift there was in his knees.

I don't know but I have curious thoughts about myself, as I was going along there, a young girl in a boy's britches, steering her mule through the twilit streets of Paris. With my gun and my knife. Didn't I feel in that peculiar moment fearless enough, a girl that should have been all fear at that time? Rended by someone and in the cold parlance of the preacher, no doubt, ruined? No girl less ruined than me. I was beginning to feel myself a very monster of courage. How did that happen? All the chill raiment of fright and doubt dropped from my shoulders. I wondered would it ever rise up from the cold earth to drape me about again?

I felt I was fit for anything, I felt I was on the cusp of great deeds.

That was because having taken in my poor six-year-old heart and found it rattling and empty Thomas and John had stuffed it up with courage.

When I stopped at the wide door of the livery I saw a pulsing light. I dismounted and went in. John Perry the blacksmith from the other side of Court Square must have dragged in his travelling forge because there he was working the bellows, so that the wind being pushed into the enclosed box swelled the flames and then by preference the flames subsided. The livery had become a huge mouth, breathing in and out with all the horror of a dragon. Frank Parkman was bent over at the hind of a fine black horse, cradling one of the hooves on his lap and knees, and with his pincers was prising out the remnant nails of a lost shoe, and with a twist of his wrist firing each one into the dark abyss of the livery. As he worked he was speaking across the void to John Perry, a huge dark man looking even huger and darker in the infernal flames and shadows, obliged indeed to shout out above the busy roars of the furnace to answer him. What they were saying I couldn't tell. Just the easy back and forth of working men. I peered about the livery, wondering had I indeed been in there before, and with no answering information coming from what I was seeing. I had no feel of dread and remembrance anyhow. Now John Perry plucked out a horseshoe with his iron grips, laid it on the ground for a moment, where it set the wet sawdust storming with smoke, drove in some kind of an iron frame, and used this to hand it to Frank Parkman, like a child offers toast on a fork. Frank Parkman gripped the hoof again and set the glowing shoe against the horn of it, so that the very bone seemed to go on fire. I was watching all this, so fascinated I nearly forgot why I was there. Then there was trimming and the using of the file, and then the fresh nails driven in anew, and then twisting and cutting and firming. My own people since they lived on endless grasses never had a need for an iron shoe. It was the iron shoe thrown in by the Yankee story had done us so much mischief, I thought. The iron shoe and all the damnable *accoutrements* that came with it.

Lana Jane Sugrue wasn't the only dame spoke bits of French.

Then the scene of fire and smoke calmed down and I suppose a great service was done the horse at least. Frank Parkman was lighting his lamps now where they hung on the great beams, and slowly the light showed more and more of the cavernous stables, and eventually showed me to Frank Parkman. He straightened up and examined me assiduously from about twenty paces off. He looked like he was thinking for a little, maybe sizing me up for danger. Or wondering, ain't I seen this Injun afore? Well, he must have decided he hadn't.

'What can I do for you, chief?' he said.

John Perry paid no heed to lamps nor Indians, and was dragging his little furnace away again into the street where he tipped it and out spilled his burning coals in a flashing leaping vee of commotion. With a wild sweep of his arm, he heaved up the furnace on a long iron bar, and swung it with amazing deftness through the air, and pitched it into one of the water troughs of the livery. There it exploded in a crazy boil of smoke and steam and

I heard John Perry laughing as if this was his favourite moment in all the ancient task of shoeing a horse. Naturally Frank Parkman and myself were obliged to wait out this violent spectacle before I could answer him.

Neither my head nor my mouth was that full of a question, I must allow. What did I want to know from him? Did Jas Jonski your good friend drag in his little Indian girl here a month back and – well, I was not even sure I had the word for the next thing. Ravish, ruin, disgrace, attack, murder, hurt, make wretched, burn bad as a heated horseshoe laid against her groin?

Chapter Eight

'Well, Cochise?' Frank Parkman said.

Behind the lights of the town continued to glimmer and enlarge in glow.

Sometimes you don't see maggots in a lump of old meat till you shift it. Now I was standing full of strange fear in a place of fear. It was the very shifting state of my poor head that was starting to confound me. Confound me in my purpose, as the lawyer Briscoe might say. How alone I was, in Thomas McNulty's trews. With a man in front of me that just wanted to slake his thirst maybe after the turmoil of shoeing that horse. I noticed again it was a beautiful, glistening black gelding. Now in the gathering light of the lamps his coat was almost leaping with the colour black.

'That some beautiful animal,' I said, suddenly able to speak.

'That sure is,' said Frank Parkman. 'Lady from Nashville came up on that. All by her lonesome. I ask you, why did she not take the Nashville train or the Mills Point stage? I ask you, stranger. Ain't fit times for a woman to be riding alone.'

'I guess,' I said.

He wasn't the Frank Parkman who had ridden out to the farm. He wasn't half smiling and half joking. He went over to a water butt and pulled out a drink in an old tin cup. It was so old the enamel was half a memory on it. Then he drew out his little clay pipe and his pouch and started to stuff the little bowl. Then he startled me and himself by striking his parlour match so trustingly that the head flew off and crossed the stables like a shooting star. Now he did laugh and cursed a little and struck another. He was eyeing the flight of the first match because he didn't want to burn down his place of work.

'This your place?' I said, though I knew it could not be.

'Yes,' he said. 'My pappy built it. Dead now, God rest him. Jesse James docked his horse here when he came with Quantrill.'

'You Jas Jonski's friend?' I said, emboldened to get another surprising answer.

'Yep, I know Jas,' he said. 'Why you ask, chief?'

'Just asking.'

'So, you just asking. No charge for that,' he said. Now he had his pipe going well and he leaned up against the old weathered centre beam of the livery and puffed away. Then he indicated the fine black horse. 'That Jas Jonski's mother's horse, as a matter of fact. Fancy. And you just asking about him.'

He smoked on for a few minutes. He was looking at me with all the easiness of friendship. It was mighty strange.

'Well, I going to close up now. I got to get my supper.'

'You leaving the horses?'

'Just for an hour. They don't mind.'

He had about fourteen or fifteen guests, all inserted into their allotted stalls.

'You can watch them if you like. I give you a fifty cents for that,' he said.

I was caught off guard by this remark. Kindness? Maybe he thought I looked like a poor scrawny Injun boy. Needed fifty cents for his own supper.

'I could do that,' I said.

'You ain't no horse thief or nothing?'

'I ain't. I got my own mule outside.'

'I saw that skinny vehicle. Anyhows. You dead right. I should never leave them. Maybe I just go fetch a pot of stew and bring it back and I can share that with you.'

I said nothing. Frank Parkman bestirred himself and put the livery doors nearly closed and winked at me and then went on his way. I was surprised again by him, that he had left me there and entrusted me with his kingdom. I was surprised and confused by his whole manner. I was glad to get the chance to look about without him being there. I was trying to get my mind to go back and tell me something. I was just not familiar with the place. Even with whiskey in my body I felt sure I would remember something just by being there. But no memory was stirring.

Again to my further astonishment Frank Parkman came back with a cuddy-bowl of stew from the chophouse. He divvied it up army fashion and gave me my share on the back of a piece of scrap metal that had a little dome hammered into it. As it happened it was excellent stew, just as good as Rosalee's.

'I thank you for sharing your food,' I said.

'Well, bible obliges us to feed the wayfarer,' he said.

'Not every soul wants to feed an Indian,' I said.

'A lot of foolish thinking afflicts the world,' he said.

Then he finished eating and went over to the doors again and pulled them shut. There was a big iron bar for a latch but he left that alone. He took my excuse for a plate and set it down and then he stood in front of me.

'I don't know if you would be kind enough to let me kiss you,' he said. He spoke very gently, very softly – very kindly.

If I was confused before I was in a maze of confusion now. Did he know who I was after all? It didn't seem so. Guess he was a man like John Cole, who didn't abhor to kiss another man. A man like John Cole, who had made it his life's work to love Thomas McNulty.

I stared back at him. Truth was, I was frightened.

'I got a knife in my boot, just so you know,' I said.

I felt the closed doors behind me with the force of an imprisonment. But I was wrong to feel that maybe.

'I got a gun too,' I said.

'If you don't care to, I don't mind one whit,' said Frank Parkman, laughing, or nearly laughing. 'If you don't ask in this world you don't get.'

'I never been kissed in my whole life,' I heard myself saying. 'I guess I should be going now.'

'Sure thing,' he said. 'You ever have a yearning to be kissed by me, you come back. Come back anyhow, anytime. You a nice soft boy.'

I nodded to him. I thought any moment he was going to turn wildcat on me and fire off a punch or something – just like the head of that lucifer. But he didn't.

I turned to go and right enough the livery doors opened easily to my touch.

'Hey, Cochise,' he said. I turned again to him just on the cusp of going out into the town. 'You not offended?'

'I ain't,' I said.

Then he nodded his head and seemed satisfied.

●

In our efforts to heal Tennyson, Thomas McNulty asked me would I mind if we boiled up some merriment that night for him. A huge swathe of the planting had now been done and it was a great weight taken off for such a long job to be nearing its ending.

'I would like that, greatly,' I said.

'Well, sweet child, so would we all,' he said. 'I am mindful, ever mindful, of what befell you, daughter.'

'I know, Mamma,' I said.

That night the floor was swept and the few sticks pushed back to the walls and Lige Magan disinterred his fiddle from the top of a cupboard and shone it up with wax and tightened his strings and off he flew with his Tennessee jigs and reels. Tennyson Bouguereau stood on the floor with face agape and he stamped his feet and applauded and hooted, and Thomas was asked to do his lady's dance that earned us our dollars in Grand Rapids if without the dress as of yore and he obliged and the room widened to the width of the firmament and our faces glowed in the lamps and there was laughter and sweating and good fellowship. Still there was not a note in the great singing bird that had been Tennyson.

I swirled and stamped as good as the next man. How I loved to swing about in a dance. I let my limbs be crazy and there was no civilised name for how I did. Not waltzing or the like. John Cole and Thomas threw me from one to the other and Rosalee like a blooming flower not just threw caution to the wind but was the wind. Her lovely body glistened and leapt and she threaded herself through the air like a lithesome black swan. Her brother stayed rooted the while but maybe we hoped the root itself would work down into the timbers and the dry earth of Tennessee and fix him.

Late in the night the way people do we settled down like horses after a long gallop and enjoyed the blazing fire and felt pretty comfortable in our dark cabin under the stars and for that while my heart was not sore and Lige Magan turned to the medicine of lullabies and laments on his fiddle and the four strings vibrated their lovely music and our hearts were full. I thought of all the woken and sleeping animals in the woods beyond and wondered if their ears were cocked to us and whether something in the music was for them too.

●

Colonel Purton made progress too – he wasn't long finding names and bringing them to the lawyer Briscoe. The lawyer Briscoe was much intrigued by Colonel Purton. It seemed to me the moment he arrived that the lawyer Briscoe delighted in him. His rank came from his days strangely enough in the butternut army but he was no rebel now and that previous governor himself of Tennessee had set him to hunting renegades. This was not a fashionable endeavour in most quarters, these days, said the lawyer Briscoe. But it seemed the colonel was going to go on doing his given duty till he was told otherwise.

'Tennessee so dangerous now,' said the colonel in a queer way of speaking that made it hard to say where he was from, 'it growing difficult to love.'

It was only then I realised that the top of the colonel's mouth was cloven because you could just see that on the lip under his fulsome moustache. That gave him the queer way of talking. Then a few moments with these words floating between us in the dark office.

'But we must continue to love it.'

So I had to think that the work of Colonel Purton was for the lawyer Briscoe a holding of things in the right direction and he was inclined to assist him in any way. Of course, it was Colonel Purton doing the assisting to him just then.

They spoke about their schooling at the Paris Male Academy which they had both attended in different years.

When folk he valued highly visited the lawyer Briscoe he was inclined to show great hospitality. He would most likely disappear into his chamber too for a little and comb and oil his hair. This for the lawyer Briscoe was the highest step of civilisation even if the smell of it only made me think of cabbages. Then he would open his finely carved cabinet where his best whiskey was kept. Even Lana Jane Sugrue, who never dropped anything because, as the lawyer Briscoe put it, she was too close to the ground, was not entrusted with the decanting and the pouring of alcohols. Maybe Colonel Purton thought he treated all his visitors likewise but it was not so. Rascals were given brief counsel and nary a glass – and then the quick exit urged by nodding and hurried words that amounted really to nonsense.

The colonel was tall, strange, and ravaged. His skin was mottled and dark, and half his face was marked by the famous port-wine stain, which gave him a peculiar double appearance, depending on which way he was facing you. I never saw a man so thin and could still be called hale. His voice was reedy and hoarse all at once, which would have been fatal to his theatrical career in Mr Noone's establishment in Grand Rapids, not to mention the harelip. But his business was not the theatre or play-acting, but the deep dangerous drama of the times.

He stood in the middle of the lawyer Briscoe's office wearing a high pair of black leather riding boots. Maybe this was why his voice was pinched so. He still wore his officer's sword, maybe for courage, or to impress his enemies. It was decorated all down its thin length with enamel the colour of lupins – the flower of my people. All in all he was wonderful and tremendous and I, though the silent Indian at the small table, felt a surge of strange optimism to view him.

'Asking questions about nightriders in Tennessee in these times,' the colonel was saying, 'used to be a fairly safe occupation. Asking questions now can get you killed quick enough. But we're in that business. We just have to know how to shoot back, I reckon.'

The lawyer Briscoe couldn't help but quietly chortle. I mean no disrespect to him by saying chortle. He was a chortler.

Then the colonel went on to describe the camp of the nightriders over at West Sandy Creek.

'I say camp but I should say city – they have built a bunch of houses there as brazen as you like, since they fear no justice now, just sitting there by the waters and the woods, and a nice warm feeling in their bellies that the world is going their way,' said the colonel. 'That what I hear about it. I ain't seen it with my own eyes.'

The lawyer Briscoe was listening without interrupting, swirling around the whiskey in his glass, so that the small lights of the room were catching in it.

'Who this boy here?' said the colonel, adverting to me, no doubt with sunken body in the corner, listening the while for clues and sparks of facts.

'This a young Sioux person of great ability,' said the lawyer Briscoe, giving me a shock of pleasure. I was happy with both ends of that opinion. 'Who keeps my books and does a damn fine job of it.'

'Too young to serve in the late war,' said the colonel in his stately manner. 'I was commissioned to command the 1st Cherokee Mounted Rifles. I bore witness to the courage and horsemanship and marksmanship of the Indian.'

The lawyer Briscoe chortled again. He liked to hear a man praise another man. It was part of his good nature.

'Many years ago,' said the lawyer Briscoe, in an effort to add to the general praise of Indians it seemed, 'this young person was obliged to shoot a member of the Tach Petrie gang. Only a child at the time, ain't that right, Mr Cole?'

'That right,' I said, blushing. Mr Cole.

'He shot him fair and square and received a wound in return.'

'Petrie?' said the colonel. 'You bring me to my business. It's Zach Petrie leads these nightriders, cousin to that late dastard Tach Petrie you mention. Aurelius Littlefair his goddamned lieutenant. And they have nigh on fifty riders. Why don't they come in from the woods? Because they have a hundred dark crimes on their heads. Murders, hangings, and ravishments. Ravishments beyond belief. The cold bare cruelty of it. Mr Cole, you may be familiar with the emperor Aurelius?'

'No, sir,' I said.

'A great philosopher of Ancient Rome. Aurelius Littlefair is no goddamned philosopher. He is a cold cruel man. Zach Petrie he be a tumultuous bear. A tumultuous bear. His claws are bared, and he desires, he desires to stir them in blood. But he ain't so black as Littlefair.'

'Colonel,' said the lawyer Briscoe, 'you reckon these men might be responsible for the attack on Tennyson Bouguereau?'

'I know they are. Sheriff Flynn was able to capture one of his boys, called Wynkle King. He was found drunk in Zollicoffer's saloon. Sheriff Flynn brought him to me. King told me everything and denied it in the morning. Too goddamned late.'

Wynkle King was another one of Jas Jonski's go-about best buddies. He had stuck in my memory because Jas Jonski had said his friend had a bladder ruined by moonshine – had to piss every thirty minutes – one of Jas Jonski's 'riotous good stories'.

'And why, Colonel, did they beat that poor man?' said the lawyer Briscoe.

'Because Bouguereau was once a slave, that all. No more nor less. A black man alone in the twilight and out of the dark trees they swoop. Hunting prey. The Petries had forty slaves to work their place – lost them all to freedom – *vain transitory splendours*. That's Goldsmith, Mr Cole.'

I was thinking he mightn't have the whole story there but his very tremendousness seemed to forbid me saying anything.

'That a cruel reason to nigh ruin a man,' said the lawyer Briscoe.

'Cruel reasons rule these times,' said the colonel, with a flourish of his dank and matted hair. 'Looking into these matters be bread-and-butter work for Sheriff Flynn. As usual as sunlight.' He had taken off his elegant hat about two speeches back and now bestrewed himself on his chair like a suit of old clothes thrown carelessly there. He had his right hand gripped on the handle of his sword, still scabbarded and splendid with its lupin-blue enamel.

'Sheriff Flynn's a good man despite his troubles,' said the lawyer Briscoe. 'Because of his troubles, maybe.'

I wanted to ask what troubles, but I didn't, and nor did the colonel. Maybe he knew already. Anyway he wasn't thinking of Sheriff Flynn and his troubles in that moment.

Chapter Nine

'They been hanging men, you know, along the five roads,' went on the colonel very quietly. It was eerie to hear him in the darkened room. 'Yes sir, the five roads that lead in and out of Paris have all seen their work. If you were a Negro, Briscoe, I would say, Walk thou not alone. Or even you, Mr Cole. For Petrie's men will take you and without a Christian thought beat you down and fit you for a rope. That a fact.'

'There are folk in Paris who don't think that's wicked,' said the lawyer Briscoe.

'There are people in Paris who don't, that's true,' said the colonel contemplatively. 'So we must proceed all to the letter of the law. Law shifts about these days too.'

Then we were almost content to have a long silence. I could nearly hear the creaking of the ropes and see the hung faces. We had seen men hung like that ourselves, I remembered, on the long journey down from Michigan. I remembered that. Thomas and John believed I was asleep but I saw it. And I thought of the soft breast of Rosalee and what a monumental soul she was. I hoped it did not disgrace a boy that I cried quiet tears in the twilight but how could I do otherwise? I was lower than Rosalee but to me she was higher than any mere God. She was the only creature who had kissed me on the lips and I thought she was the carrier of the mercy of angels.

Then there was the solemn question of what Colonel Purton was going to do about things. It was such a maze of death and difficulty. In a certain way, he said, with equal solemnity, he understood the likes of Zach Petrie. Old rebels like him could vote again now in their own country but they had grown used to havoc and slaughter. Petrie had a violent sense of a man who was wronged, and he was cradling that to his chest evermore, said the colonel. The lawyer Briscoe silently agreed. I could sense in all they said the danger, the sorrow. As a child of sorrow I could hear the under-songs in what they spoke of. The fall of things that had been precious, the rise of trouble and the taking away of joys. It was one of those strange times when I understood the whiteman better. That in his own sphere of suffering he was not unlike myself, though he might scream at me for saying so. He had no good word for Aurelius Littlefair, who he said again was a bandit of the blackest heart. Wynkle King half said and half didn't say, avowed the colonel, that it was Aurelius Littlefair struck down Tennyson with a billhook with an intent not just to kill but to cut off his head. But Zach Petrie had a different fame. You could hear in the colonel's voice a grudging respect. And I remembered the curious care that Thomas McNulty had given the grave of his brother Tach, dug after all not twenty feet from Lige's cabin. An adversary of the most atrocious sort, and yet . . . As for a boy like Wynkle King, he was only a drunkard with a drunkard's tongue and a dicky bladder.

But Zach Petrie had lost a whole world.

In Tennessee, said the colonel, there were thousands of aggrieved souls like Zach Petrie. Men so disgruntled by the war they couldn't breathe the air of peace, it choked them. And were such that no new times could please them, no matter how close they came to what they had fought for.

'You let them make an army of themselves again, what we have so far will be only to have sown the wind,' said the colonel. 'We will reap the whirlwind.'

'And the city shall be taken, and the houses rifled, and the women ravished,' said the lawyer Briscoe. 'Zechariah, 14:2.'

'Zach Petrie, 1874,' said Colonel Purton.

The lawyer Briscoe laughed, but there was a faltering beat to the laughter. He replenished the colonel's glass as if in tribute to his wit nonetheless. The colonel acknowledged the gesture by raising the glass to us both. The purple face, the ruptured lip. Then they seemed more content with silence. But creatures who know each other may be very talkingly silent.

'Sir, may I ask, what will you do?' I said.

'We must ride against him,' said the colonel. 'I'll lead my men down here at daybreak.'

'Do we have the laws to do that?' said the lawyer Briscoe.

'I'll bring the papers required,' said the colonel.

'May the Lord protect us,' said the lawyer Briscoe.

●

That night I was in sore need of Rosalee's closeness. I felt battered by the colonel's elegant talk. I felt small and lightless. What was my injury beside this teeming history? And yet lying with Rosalee, as slowly the heat of her body leaked into me, I returned to a sense of myself. An injury to one soul might be of small account in the great and endless flower-chain of human injuries. But was not the law designed to peer at each, one by one, and give everything equal weight betimes? This I had learned from the lawyer Briscoe. It seemed to be a curing truth. Rosalee was curled about my back, I was pressed into the C she made of her body, and made another close-written C in the darkness. Our coverings were scant and threadbare. Her breast was so warm it felt like wings on my back.

•

Thomas McNulty, John Cole, and Lige Magan had risen and gone out to their labours as the owls were going to bed and the farm was still in its clothes of darkness and silence. How lonesome the things in the parlour looked without its people. The rough old table, the antlers holding the battered hats, the picture of Polk on the wall. Lige Magan had set himself to put in four acres of corn, just, he said, 'to jump the muscles another way'. I had not seen them the night before either. I had looked for them but they had long since crept to their rest. Planting corn was a hammer to wakefulness.

And there was a great caution in me against speaking to them. If I had seen them I would have been obliged to speak, for the sake of honesty. It was the easily torn spider's web of what we were that gave me disquiet. Old soldiers of the Union army but also a deserter and a freedman. I didn't want them torn from their farm on my account.

But my foolish thought or the thought I had considered foolish – to do something about things myself – had planted itself. It gave me strength to notice strength in myself. Like a small slim lucifer gives fire to greater fire.

A Tennessee mule is not a small creature. I was happy when Tennyson Bouguereau appeared in the gloom of the stable- house and helped me saddle up. Great heaving and grunting but never a word. I told him where I was hoping to go that day, and I explained to him why. I told him everything that the colonel had said and Tennyson gave every sign of understanding for he stood there amazed at my words. Just as I might have declared, in cold judgement of the world I knew, he didn't believe any Christian alive thought it was wrong to hurt him. That no court, no lawyer, and no lawman would think it was so. And yet he was hearing my speech.

He might be having trouble making sounds but he wasn't having the least trouble hearing them.

He turned out a stirrup for me and I stood in near. I was so close to him that I smelled the hyacinth on his skin. He smiled at me with his barn-wide smile. I knew he didn't think I was a cur of an Indian, not at all. He knew what I was. He knew what we were. Proper souls just waiting on some never-coming dawnlight, some sort of soul anyhow.

I hoiked up my foot and lodged it in the stirrup. He got his shoulder under my backside. Just before he performed that kindness, he gripped my free hand and didn't shake it but veritably squeezed it.

Now I could believe myself to be on righteous duty in the service of Tennyson Bouguereau, if also secretly myself. He hoisted me into the saddle. Then in dumb show he bid me wait while he went to fetch something. All this in sign language like Indians themselves sometimes do.

He was back in a trice and strapped an old holster to the mule and shoved in his Spencer rifle. He lashed on a square of ripped burlap to hide it.

He was a handsome, tidy man. An emperor. What was that good man's name that the colonel had mentioned? He was an *Aurelius*.

It was that time of morning I guess when folks liked to stir along the road. Serving girls going into town with baskets, some barefoot and some in dusty shoes. The dawn had brought the quiet trees forth in their black garb. And farmers I half knew drawing great carts of things, bushels fastened with twisted straws, baskets frothing green with the spring harvest. A high long tobacco cart, carrying other freight the while, thundered by. It had been a courtesy to greet everyone you passed in former days, even for an Indian person. But not in those days. The fulgent sunlight belied the frosty eyes that glanced at me. Little groups of Negroes passed along, whether local workers or wanderers I couldn't know. It was as if every heart was dumbstruck. I kicked along my mule, glad of the rifle slugging in its holster. The burlap had slipped sideways and the sunlight flashed off the breechblock, as if to say, be wary, be watchful of this rider.

●

The lawyer Briscoe's yards teemed with horses and mules. A bubbling stew of necks and tossing heads. Colonel Purton and his lieutenants were shouting orders and I could hear them from back along the road. The militia were like a big haberdashery of blue cloth, just like real Union soldiers, but sometimes a jaunty hat flew about like a fancy bird. Mostly young men, with a hungry look to them. The lawyer Briscoe was on his front stoop, taking papers from the colonel, and writing away at other papers lying before him. It looked like they were going to have everything trim to the law, in best lawyer Briscoe fashion. I felt slight and thin in my clothes but Tennyson's rifle gave me at least a sense of extra bulk.

I lopped my reins at a spare pole and walked up to the stoop as casually as I could. Just to look like I was arriving to work. Now I could see that on some of the papers were lists of names, no doubt the roll call of the gathered boys.

'I am supposing, Colonel, we still under the shelter of the Calling Forth Act as regards this militia.'

'Damned if I know,' said the colonel, 'anyhow, we called forth, and that a fact.'

'We have seventeen hangings petitioned against Petrie's men and we have so many burnings and killings and we have one of his own men in drunkenness attesting to the most brutal and foul assault on Mr Tennyson Bouguereau, freedman of this county.'

'That the cent makes a dollar of this,' said the colonel. 'I ain't got no qualms, we ride forth because we called forth by law and justice. I have countersigned that order of the town commissioners and they got that paper from goddamned state legislature or some other gaggle of geese. What more can civilisation do for us?'

'Nothing,' said the lawyer Briscoe. And he signed off his last paper with a flourish. I knew that among his many weighty titles he was commissioner for the railroad and I supposed he was some other mighty thing for the militia too. No kindness and no cruelty in white-eye America was ever done without a piece of paper somewhere tipped in. Even an Indian girl like me bobbed up to look like a clean-faced boy knew that. All my people had been killed clean to the letter of the law, I did not doubt. Not our law, but our law was just words on the wind.

'I got a lieutenant here knows the exact spot where they gathered,' said the colonel. I was noticing that any letter of the alphabet that needed his tongue to touch the top of his mouth gave off little explosions. 'Where a little creek called Beasley enters the West Sandy Creek. Well, we got a three-hour ride so we best be riding.'

And he swung away with his thin face and his scarecrow body and even by just stirring seemed to gather his men to themselves so that somehow out of a moiling mess of mounted riders he pulled them into a perfect column two deep on the narrow road. I stood by the lawyer Briscoe's watching head. He was tapping the table with his pen. It had done its work and the work he could do in this enterprise. And I counted them going out his gate and got to all of two hundred. I remembered the colonel saying that Petrie had fifty followers so maybe that would make a great ruinous flood of men against him.

The lawyer Briscoe was a wise old man. He didn't even look round at me.

'You coming now to work?' he said. 'I think you ain't.'

'I have a little business over by Beasley Creek,' I said.

'I think you do,' said the lawyer Briscoe.

●

My mule was pulling the reins and fretting on his tether because the yards had emptied of his kind and he was anxious to follow. So was I, though not a man among them was my kind, that was true. Anyhow I trotted out onto the Huntingdon road and followed the long column at a distance of two, three hundred yards. A long way back so the outriders wouldn't pay me heed.

Who was that small person seeking justice? I cannot say. As I trotted along I told myself over and over the legend of my mother's courage. But was this an instance of courage in me, or reckless folly?

The column streamed eastward. A high cold sky was speckled with stray blues and greys like a bird's egg. But a reluctant sunlight was trying to measure the height of the sky with long thin veins. I supposed I could measure it in feet and yards myself if I had a ladder high enough. But what was it to know such things? Was the sum of what my mother said not of more use to me? That if I persisted, if I went on far enough, in good faith, I would reach her again alive. I would reach my sister, and my aunts, I would find all the medicine of my people's love, all the to-and-fro and majesty of their lives.

I rode along less fearful than I might have been. I was thinking. If Jas Jonski was the heart of it, this was just so many miles off that centre. My quest to avenge myself had leaped a wall into that further place that contained the justice of Tennyson. I thought I could work my way back too if I had to. I thought I could attend to this, as the lawyer Briscoe might say, and then leap the boundary again on a lithesome pony of thought.

And do so not because it was blind folly but because my mother had shown me how to shuck off fear and have the courage of a thousand moons.

Chapter Ten

Maybe some of those militia boys had Indian grandmothers too because they took to the tracks that bordered farms and then picked their way through the wooden hills by trails so faint I thought only an Indian could see them. Now the column had lengthened by a measure of two as they settled into single file. I had all the secrecy of the first budding trees now. I could follow the chink-chank of the militia's progress and all the other small sounds of metal and horses. Not too much Indian about that cacophony but it might have served for the likes of Zach Petrie's men, with all the strange deafness of whitemen. Young birds sparkled up out of the underbrush. You could sense the ten thousand eyes of animals that must have noted our passing through easily enough. Noted and kept back, kept quiet. The trees were not so high hereabouts, they looked like things that had grown back after old clearances. The farms themselves looked strange and dirty, though all good land I knew, and even all these years after the war there were stretches of it with the memory of blackening and levelling as old revengeful rebels had gone through. Jesse James himself the famous robber had been through all this country with Quantrill, just as Parkman said. Fences were still down in many places and the cabins themselves black as the throats of chimneys. Even ten years after the war. Maybe each burned farm was a Union soul, and each let thrive a Confederate. If there were crops set in it was corn and tobacco mostly. Just like out on the big roads, few figures in the fields waved a greeting. Some did. That nice lazy hat-waving of Tennessee farmers. I was seeing all this from my allotted distance. Most often the trees were scraggy though they hid the militia from view. Suddenly I would see them, pushing on. Soldiers going to a fight have a special air. It's not their usual covering of distances. I remembered my uncle's men leaping onto their horses and going away from the camp just like that. Sort of sombre and gay at the same time. Expectant and maybe frightened, a little. I thought, how strange and good that my astonishing mother had gone with them, now and then. To raid or rattle an enemy. To take horses, to take women too. To kill with a fierce and honest hunger. To persist, to last, out there on the plains.

Boys called nightriders might be expected to be found in their beds by day. Now here was the little city told of to the colonel lying up on a clearing by the old river. I was halted on a wooded rise above the scene. A smaller creek rattling in on gleaming dark stones made a ford of the main creek below the cabins. I kept off with my three hundred paces but I could no longer see the colonel's men. They had maybe crept down into the small oaks tangling up the riverbank on this side. It was difficult to see. The aspect of the so-called city – just in truth a half dozen ramshackle throw-ups – was strangely serene. There was a clutch of toiling women washing big white sheets upriver. They were hitting the twisted cloth against the black rocks and even from a distance I could see the dirty suds fleeing downriver like so many waterbirds. I could even hear the voices of the women talking, chatting away, seemingly as happy as ever women were to be together at such tasks. The work eased by gossip and laughter. I felt a sort of sorrow to see it. Not only because it put me in powerful mind of our own Lakota village in the long ago but because I was an Indian girl who could never have spoken so at ease with those laughing women. Their dresses hitched to their waists and their legs gleaming wet. Helpless, happy laughter. No certificate of travel could gain me entry there, and I was sorry for it. There was an enchantment in it that burned into me, though I was stilled there on my mule ready to go down and do them perchance mischief. I sat in my manly clothes and longed for something I had no lingo for, English or Indian. I don't know even now what that was.

As I thought these curious thoughts suddenly the undergrowth erupted with riders below me. The colonel cried out an order and raising his sword plunged down onto the ford, deep enough where he entered. He was giving room to his eager men behind. The ford might have been two feet deep with a strong sluggish water on it. The horses' legs were slowed, the men hallooed and kicked forward, the river was trying to gainsay them. Out of the cabins indeed in their nightshirts blossomed the sleepy nightriders. It was that moment when two stories come together: the story of what the colonel wanted to do, and the story of those dreaming men. And to join them required that cacophony and turmoil. Eagerness and sleepiness made all the one in the boil of the moment. They had no sentries set it would seem. All was surprise and havoc and calling. A big man had run out from a cabin and was standing now in the centre of their rough compound, his nightdress billowing like a dismantled teepee, roaring orders. Big raging roaring loud-bellowed orders that the distance made almost comical. The women washing sheets leaped from the water like the petals of an exploded flower and their dresses dropped long to their ankles and I thought I could see them gathering rifles into their clutches. Now rifles and guns began to fire with a violent *pock-pock* though I stood so far away. I saw the fiery flashes. I kicked my mule forward.

As the little trail went down it entered a deep stand of trees and I couldn't see the cabins now. Though I thought I was keeping them square to my face even so when I came out of the trees again I was fifty yards downriver of the mayhem. I saw bodies lying on the river meadow and I saw others wounded maybe dragging themselves to whatever safety could be devised and I saw Colonel Purton's men storm the far bank with a tremendous fusillade and some with repeating rifles were riding Indian style without reins and working the breechblock and the trigger with both hands and firing, firing as if God had ordained this fury of firing. No effort had been made to get surrender from these men. No surrender maybe thought likely. It was smother them with the force of numbers, two hundred men against fifty souls, batter into them with a three-sided sickle of horses, engulf, dismay, destroy. The smoke of gunpowder rose from the melee. It might have been a clement morning mist along the peaceful river only for the great caterwauling of voices and the horrible screeching of wounded horses. I had seen just this before, but from inside a Sioux village. Inside the terror, at the heart of it. And everything I loved up to that moment about to be cancelled off the earth. As if bogus lives. Kill them all! And I sat there astride the mule like someone not there at all, but somewhere else, somewhere far away on the plains of Wyoming, but also, someone exactly there, living, gasping for breath, terrified. Then this strange girl came blazing from the undergrowth, dressed so vividly in a bright yellow dress that even in my great fright I noted it, bringing up her musket as if it was part of her own body, as if it had her own blood running through it in veritable veins, and fired it at my body. I felt the bullet tear into my right arm, I was only half leaning down to the Spencer rifle, I was just on the point of grasping it, when the bullet battered into my arm, battered into it, and I hauled up the Spencer, I knew the bullet was sitting in its little grave, and I fired blindly, something rose through me like a fire, my own blood was burning, it was the fiery pain of battle, and the pain pitched me down into blackness. No, no, now I was awake again, wide-eyed. That was a strange quick blackness. Did a minute pass? A moment? My enemy was now lying out across a riverside bush, also very strangely. I didn't know if I had killed her. Or even shot her. I couldn't see blood. She was a black-haired dark-skinned girl so beautiful the creek below wanted her. Her two legs remained on the bank, but the whole rest of her was depending on the kindness of that bush not to drop her down. Her head was furthest away, only four feet from the surging creek, which was full of spring rain. She was trying to bend back to safety with her two arms outstretched. We could hear the kerfuffle of the battle upriver still going on.

'Hey, mister,' she said.

'What?'

'Suppose you could grab my hand?' she said.

'You shot me,' I said, and I could see my own blood trickling down from my shoulder, though not as much as I expected.

'I did,' she said, 'but, I can't swim.'

'Maybe you best drown then,' I said.

Then the bush lurched down an inch, two inches.

'Jeez Christ,' she said, and closed her eyes. 'Hey, mister?'

'What?'

'Sorry I shot you.'

'If I save you now maybe you go and get your rifle and shoot me again.'

'As God my witness, I undertake – I ain't never going to shoot you again. My rifle done fell in the river. Please, mister, take my hand.'

'I ain't no mister,' I said.

'I know, you just a boy.'

I planted my boots on the edge of the bank and leaned over to grab her right hand. Then I had her hand in my hand. It struck me that she might be tricking me and about to drag me in with her. There was quietness upriver now, except for some hallooing, and the sound of horses scrabbling up scree. I hauled on her. She was so light she came easily, but the bush was against her intention, and down she spilled into the current, her yellow dress starting quickly to sink and drag her to her doom. She let out a screech like a hawk going down on its prey. But I had her fast. She got her boots back on the slippery earth, and was like a person running for their life, her legs blading and flashing with effort. With all my strength I dragged her up, and then sat down abruptly myself. I had hauled her back with my injured arm and it was a daisy of a pain now.

'You took a bullet?' I said.

'I took no bullet,' she said. 'I took a big fright. That a big noisy gun you got.'

Then she lay on her side panting. She was like a pony that had galloped a few miles too far.

'Thank you – *boy*.'

'I ain't no boy either,' I said. I didn't even know why. What was it to her if I was a girl or a boy? A girl herself attached most forcibly to a gang of marauding killers. But I did say it.

'What you?' she said.

'I a girl,' I said. 'Winona.'

◐

She undertook then as a mere kindness or a thank you for saving her skin to walk back along the way with me.

I didn't know how to get back to any road otherwise. She stuck the offending Spencer back into its holster. She took the reins and led the weary mule.

'Guess we had our own private battle back there,' she said, but this didn't seem to need a reply.

I couldn't detect any sign of the militia. It was late afternoon towards evening now and there were whippoorwills that side of the county too by all accounts. I told her who the men were that I had ridden in with and whenever there was a gap in the trees or the ground rose somewhat, she would go up on her tippy toes and try and get a view back towards her wickiup village. She didn't seem anxious about anything now. If it had been Lige Magan's place I would have been hurrying back and damn any girl, bullet or no. I could almost see the yellow dress drying on her what with the Godgiven heat in her body.

'Well, I'll be,' she said.

'What do you mean?'

'Don't think Zachary Petrie were expecting *that*.'

'You someone's daughter?'

'I *someone's* daughter. Ain't everyone?'

'Someone in that camp?'

'I Peg,' she said. 'My mother were riding with Quantrill, you know? She dead a long time. She were a camp woman. My father were a scout for Quantrill. He dead too.'

'You Indian?' I said. That would make sense, I thought – with the dark hair and dark skin and the – the beauty of her.

'I am. What, you don't like Injuns?'

She knew well what I was. It was meant to be humorous. It was. We both laughed. But it's painful to laugh with a bullet wound in your arm.

Then she found a new gap and went up on her tippy toes again.

'Mercy me,' she said, mostly to herself. 'I don't think he were expecting *that*.'

For some reason too dark for me to understand she was the kind of person you might be inclined to tell things to. Don't ask me why. So I told her all my trouble and I felt a damn sight better for doing so. And I told her about Jas Jonski and how dark all *that* was. She was pensive for a long time, and then she said:

'I guess he done it alright.'

This I heard with a strange interest but I didn't have long to ponder it. We came round a huge mossy boulder and there on the ground was a big black bear. She must have been three hundred pounds in weight. Round as the same boulder and black as a kettle. Well you don't go trying to shoot a creature like that, you got to scare her away. A huge head swung to look at Peg, still leading the mule. Their noses, her nose, the bear's nose, and the mule's nose, were not three feet apart. The mule didn't like that, no more did Peg. A black bear is a softer soul than those grizzlies out on the western plains. A grizzly likes to attack first and think later, if bears do think. But this bear had that taken-aback look, closely matched by Peg's. It was a tricky situation for the bear. Who to express anger to first? The mule reared up and down I came like a sack of sweet corn. Peg raised her arms and roared, trying to scare off the great animal. Then I stood at her side and roared too. The movement forward seemed to decide the bear. Or maybe it was my blood she smelled. She swung a paw at me so quick it seemed not possible to avoid it. A claw caught in Thomas's old trews and took them off me like they were a dress. Maybe they weren't too solid in the first place. Now I was naked as a child from waist to boots. The mule backed off and Peg forgot to let go – she was dragged back ten feet in the beat of a moment. I roared and leaped about, that was what you had to do, bears don't like you to stand your ground. Not to their liking. An ignorant person might have tried to use the musket. I could have sworn she looked at me deep in the eyes for a long long minute. Maybe I imagined that. She could have killed me easily enough. Crashed after Peg, killed her, and just as nimbly could have killed my poor mule, now in a panic the size of a barn. As suddenly as we had come upon her, she was gone, leaving an enormous dark clamorous space where she had been, like an after image in the eye.

I expected to see a long cut from that claw but there wasn't a scratch on me. I was gazing down at my naked legs. Peg calmed the mule and tied him and I am sure was also expecting a wound beyond her management. But I was whole, save the bullet wound still seeping into my shirt, now my only item of clothing. The trews were ruined, they had ripped from the crotch right down the legs, both sides, you could have used them as a raggedy sail.

We were shaken. But the world was full of bears all told and why should we be amazed? Peg looked at me and caught my eye and she laughed again. She had bent down to pick up my little pearly pistol and was handing it to me. She started with a little trickle of laughter and then she was laughing like a drunk in Zollicoffer's. I hoped the bear didn't think we were laughing at her.

'You can't go up on the road like that,' said Peg, 'you just can't.'

I was horrified at the thought. To ride even in the darkness naked to my boots. With a dozen men to pass. I didn't look like a boy now, it was plain to see.

Suddenly Peg was pulling off her yellow dress.

'Give me your shirt,' she said. 'I need your shirt.'

'What you doing?' I said.

'I ain't got to show my modesty but to these trees,' she

said. 'I'll take you to the road and then turn myself for home.'

She stood now in the starry darkness, in only a pair of scanty bloomers.

'Give me the bloomers,' I said. 'You can keep your dress.'

'I ain't sending you home in bloomers,' said Peg. 'Put it on.'

So I took off the shirt, groaning a little I will allow, and gave it to her and then I drew on the yellow dress. Luckily the dress had no arms or I would never have got it over the wound. We were the same sort of shape so it fitted as though it were my own. I found a good pocket for the señorita gun. Then she picked up the trews and wrapped them around her waist, as some sop to decency.

'Guess you got the best part of the bargain.' Then she contemplated me for a few moments. 'Guess you a girl now right enough,' she said.

Now I could feel the weakness leaking into me from the bullet wound. She helped me back up on the shaken mule, and myself and the mule shook along together.

When she got me up nearly onto the eastern road to Paris she gave me back the reins and looked at me. I was near to fainting. In some distress I dismounted. There was so much blood from my arm now. The wound had suddenly decided to bleed copiously. She tore a length of cloth off the ruined trews, and wrapped it round the wound and pulled it tight. Her eyes intentful, even fearful. She didn't say anything else, and helped me mount again. Then she nodded her head and turned around, and went back the way she had come.

Chapter Eleven

Once out on the road alone with the light now giving up the ghost and the torn blankets of dark and half-dark falling everywhere, I started to feel that wound like all soldiers must after a few hours pass. The first rush of strength subsiding and the pain growing ever more violent and netherworld, until you wonder you never gave greater thanks every moment of your life that had passed without such a burden. It weighed me down with its strange sense of violation and awfulness. It was a disgusting thing, the mealy-mouthed cousin of courage. I had no sensations in me other than it, it hurried everything else away, claiming me as its own. Only the pain, only the pain. Then when I got right to the middle of the pain, I couldn't even breathe there. My chest was full of gasps. The road waved from side to side like a great run of water in a deep culvert. The browns of night mixed eagerly with the new blacks coming down. Every star was a shooting star. The moon rolled about prodigiously. Then everything was total black, total pain. I was half fallen from the mule because my spine had turned to cotton. I had my cheek against the mule's muscled neck. If I was dying I wondered would I bear the same pain in the land of Death, would I carry it over, would it come with me greedily? Wanting me so much it couldn't leave me? I heard a queer music along the trees and lifted my head with great weariness and stared but there was nothing there to make that sound. I thought I must be dying because a molten gold light seeped out of the black woods. It was like a huge creature. It took me and burned me in a golden bluster of pain. I saw my mother walking across the gold, her legs in golden grass. My heart burst forth from my chest like a hare, happy with love, and raced towards her. I had escaped my suffering body and soon I would be in her arms.

◐

When I woke to the world again every last speck of the gold had evaporated and my mother no doubt returned to her ancient story, beyond my ever reaching her. I thought I knew the room where I lay but could not tell exactly where it was – in what house or district. The walls were bare wooden boards and the bed was a little narrow iron thing. A small window entertained a dismal light. I heard a cock crowing some way off, and the sound of carts passing distantly outside, and the muffled underwater sound of folk going about their business – all many yards off, I thought. I was as weak as a newborn child. But with waking, fears awoke too. I fished down along my clothes for my little lady's gun but it was nowhere on my person. I was looking for the waist of my trews. Of course, I thought, I am in Peg's dress. That bear sent my pearly gun flying. But hadn't Peg handed it back to me? Was I still in my boots? No, I was barefoot now. No knife either.

Then the door opened and Jas Jonski entered, followed by a ghostly gentleman with a big leather bag. The ghostliness was only an impression maybe, but given greater force by the sudden flood of dread that engulfed me to see Jas. Worse than that bear. The very truth of the matter was, my body was terrified of him, even if my mind would not show me why. My desire to fly, to flee, was infinite. If I had not been so weary I would have been grateful to be allowed to burst out through the flimsy walls. I saw in my inner eye the planks fall down and the people outside gasp at my wondrous escape. This failure to attain freedom wrenched at me, but my body became so still I suddenly entertained the idea I was indeed dead. That Jas Jonski had only my killed body in his keeping and that the ghostly gentleman was the undertaker Luther Carp. No person that saw Luther Carp in the streets of Paris could fail to have a shiver go through them.

But this person was not Luther Carp and I was disappointed in my hopes of death.

When I tried to speak, I knew instantly that it was a mere whisper. I was dismayed by my lack of strength. I tried again.

'Thomas McNulty will be looking for me,' I said, but I might as well have remained silent, for all the effect it had on these two men.

'Thomas McNulty will be . . .'

'This Winona Cole,' said Jas Jonski, looking at me, but I thought, I know who I am – 'she found on the Nashville wagon road. Bullet wound, see?'

'She ain't nothing but an Injun,' said the man, doubtfully.

'I pay you,' said Jas Jonski, roughly.

'Injuns don't take well to medicine,' he said, so I knew he was a doctor. 'I as likely kill her as cure her. They like wild things. Ever try to fix a robin's broken leg? Same thing.'

'Look, doc, you got to get that bullet out of her and if you kill her, I kill you, how about that?'

But he wasn't saying it with menace, it was his effort to be humorous. Always the humorous boy.

'I guess that fair,' said the doc, sitting near me and opening his bag at his feet.

'You speak English?' he said.

But I said nothing.

'She speaks English. She work for the lawyer Briscoe. She civilised right enough.'

'My name is Dr Memucan Tharpe,' he said slowly, emphasising his words like you would for a child. 'And if you lie quietly there I will try and dig this bullet out of your shoulder.'

So then he was taking up a metal pliers and he put it against the wound. 'It pretty red around this hole, when she get this?'

'I was told by the men that brought her in that she was at the fight at Zach Petrie's place. They saw her follow them all the way. They were coming back with their own wounded and thought it best to put her on the cart. One of them knew she was my fiancée.'

'I weren't called to that, thank God. I heard there was a big fight,' said Dr Tharpe. 'Your fiancée? Why would you go marrying an Injun, son? They ain't got no proper understanding of that institution, believe me. Easy come, easy go.'

He had just uttered these words when he inserted his instrument to locate the hard bullet in the flesh. All I could do was take refuge in my idea of honour and not let a sound escape my lips. But if he had touched my heart with a flame it could not have been more painful.

'She don't even cry out. These creatures,' he said, 'you

see, they ain't even human, not truly, not the same as you and me.'

He found the bullet all the same and was a few moments digging in to grip it and then he drew it out with a sucking of flesh.

'Musket ball,' he opined, holding it up to the light, such as it was. 'You boil me up some water now, son, and I'll clean this off with bromine. There now, missy,' he said, touched by a pride in his work despite it was just me benefiting from it. 'Guess you'll be feeling better by and by.'

'Dr Tharpe,' I whispered, when Jas Jonski had left to go fetch the water.

'Yes, missy?' he said.

'You know Lige Magan? Elijah Magan? He got a place near McKenzie?'

'I know Lige. I knew all his people. You the little Injun living there? I heard of you too.'

'I the Injun. Doctor, can you let Lige know where I be? He sure be worried. How long I lying here? He don't know where I be.'

'Cannot young Mr Jonski do that service for you?'

'I ain't no fiancée of Jas Jonski. I a prisoner. If you can get a . . .'

Just then, the same Jas Jonski reappeared with a steaming bowl of water. The doctor looked at me and I looked at him. I didn't know what he was thinking.

'All right, missy,' he said, and smiled at Jas Jonski, and now with a somewhat gentler hand, since we were acquainted and had spoken English together, cleaned out the wound, and poured in the bromine from a little brown bottle.

'Going to have to suture this up for you, missy,' he said. 'Might hurt a little.'

Then he threaded a big needle like a very seamstress and gripped the wound. He dipped the metal in once, twice, thrice, through my skin and then his work seemed to be done. Even in this bath of pain I was desperate for fear that he would rise and leave me with Jas Jonski.

'Doctor,' I whispered again, and weakly gripped his wrist.

'Don't you fret, missy,' he said. 'You'll heal good.'

But whatever sort of man Jas Jonski was, he had a sort of instinct about him which was why I had liked him in the first place. He could see into a little problem.

'You maybe want this by you, Winona,' he said, taking out my pearly gun and placing it beside me on the bed. 'Didn't want you lying on it and shooting yourself.'

'Where my boots?' I said, in my tiny whisper.

'Where your?' he said.

'My boots.'

'Boots under your bed. And the knife is in the left one.'

'You got the Spencer rifle?'

'Didn't see no Spencer. Ain't you armed enough now?' he said, laughing.

Then they both went out. I heard the click of the lock.

◐

The curious thing that assailed me as I lay there was a worry about Tennyson's Spencer. That coveted gun which was the only precious thing that Tennyson owned. Was it lying out on the goddamn eastern road? And what of my poor mule? And would Thomas McNulty and John Cole be scouring the countryside for a trace of me? That was a better thought. I also thought, Jas Jonski is crazy to take me prisoner. There'll be veritable hell to pay for this. How great a fool I had been. Going off after soldiers like I was a true boy. Oh, but was I not the niece of a great leader, and the daughter of a warring woman? Then I was thinking, God help Jas Jonski, but the next chance I got I would kill him myself. I imagined locating my boots and plucking out my little knife and sticking it suddenly into him when he was leaning in near. Leaning in near. What right by the laws of Blackstone's book, the lawyer Briscoe's bible, did he have to take me and keep me? And I thought of Peg's words, the words of a girl I barely knew but who I had said everything to, a little waterfall and deluge. She had weighed my words as we moved among the trees and the little farms and she had concluded that Jas Jonski was a villain. And even as I raged against Jas Jonski I thought about Peg and how she had seemed to me, how strangely bright she had seemed to me, as she balanced in the bush above the murderous waters. And how, going against very nature and natural justice, I had not let her fall, I had pulled her back to life.

And then I worried again about Tennyson's rifle. You can take a bullet out of a girl's shoulder but that won't make her well. I was plunging down into fever, I knew I was. Because that strange gold creature was piercing me again, putting bright bars of light between the poor planks of the room. I thought it must be that my eyes were too open, or my head, or wherever were the doors into a person. The light crept into the room and held me pincered down in the bed. But I didn't have chains on me, I didn't have ropes. Could I not rise up if I gathered myself? Could I not call out? But I had no voice for calling out, I had no legs to raise me up.

◐

Was it a fever of hours or a fever of minutes? I had no notion of it. Except, Jas Jonski did not return.

As I pitched about in pain and confusion I almost

prayed he would. Just to stop the room spinning. Round and round as though I was strapped to a mill wheel. My stomach was burning, my wound was burning, my head was burning. Sweat sat up on my bare arms in pearly beads. Where I wasn't fire I was liquid.

Perhaps I slept. Perhaps I woke. Perhaps I slept. And woke.

Then John Cole came and took me up in his arms and carried me out. He didn't utter a word.

Lige Magan's blessed cart was waiting at the back of Mr Hicks's store. My mule was tethered to the rear. Never was human so glad to see an animal. He stamped about as if rebuking me for leaving him. Thomas McNulty was standing in the bed of the cart looking as fussed as a mother hen. I tried to see, I tried to see if the rifle was in the holster, but John Cole was lifting me up now to Thomas McNulty.

'I sorry,' I said, 'I always causing you trouble.'

I was laid down gently, just like Tennyson before me. Thomas wrapped his old army coat about me. Again, not speaking a word.

It was dark night but I saw Dr Tharpe on the boardwalk. As the cart pulled away he lifted a hand in farewell.

◐

It was so dark out on the Huntingdon road that even owls were hushed. I was the weakest girl in Tennessee but I was so happy to be held by Thomas McNulty even if he was offering me a continuous homily that included many an anguished outbreak of annoyance.

'You best hush a little, Thomas, she not ready to be rebuked,' said John Cole.

'I ain't rebuking her, I just . . .'

My voice was still vexed by extinction but I tried my best to comfort him.

'You right,' I said. 'I the greatest fool girl ever lived.'

'You not that, no, that ain't what I meaning, goddamn it, I meaning . . . You're the most precious item we got and then we find your mule wandering like a poor Ahasuerus all out of sorts and snorting lonesome fire. And then that top hat fool, what was his name, John Cole?'

'Who name?' said John Cole.

'Fool stuttering doctor full of nonsense talk?'

'That Tharpe,' said John Cole. 'Why you say that? He talked pretty good. And then we knew where Winona at. You should be baking tarts for Tharpe, Thomas.'

'Goddamn tarts, I don't know. And then we hear the worst thing we ever hear in a long long history of worst things we endured that that goddamn fool jester of a boy Jas Jonski got you – holy murdering God but what sort of news was that for us to hear? And now you saying you crept away and was following Purton and that you was in battle out at Petrie's?'

'Whyever you elect to go and do that, Winona, child?' said John Cole.

'Because Tennyson need to be righted,' I said, with words so quiet I don't believe even I could hear them. But they could hear me right enough. They had been listening to my least words all my life. They had ears for me.

They didn't say anything then. Those two men had a very profound sense of justice maybe as deep as the lawyer Briscoe's. Maybe deeper, because it arose from the heart not just Blackstone's book. I couldn't hear my own words but I could almost hear their brains working away at thoughts like little engines.

'I guess we only got ourselves to blame, John Cole,' said Thomas in some despair.

'Guess that right,' said John Cole.

Chapter Twelve

Now we heard in the distance behind us a strange rattling jangling noise, like a cart coming after us at crazy speed. It was difficult to see back the road especially for me, but John and Thomas pulled their rifles out from under John's feet. They were going to square up against the back gate of the wagon if needs be, I knew. I lifted my head as best I could and stared back down the road. It was something breathing lights and flames and making a great bluster of noise. There were a butcher's dozen of men actually pulling this vehicle, pulling and hallooing. Now I gazed up the road the other way because some other light drew my attention. The terrifying light of leaping flames that disturbs the dreams of all house dwellers. Now the charging men with their roaring vehicle passed us, not even inclined to look at us. They wore uniforms and moustaches and big tin hats.

'What news?' called Thomas. He was looking for news now. But the men said nothing in reply. Their machine looked heavy and violent. On they drew it. Two of those dapper gents were Negroes.

'They heading for the lawyer Briscoe's house,' said John Cole astutely, peering into the darkness at the distant flames.

'That not good news neither,' said Thomas.

◐

We came near to the lawyer Briscoe's and sure enough his lovely old house was ablaze. The tin-hatted boys had reached it and by some miracle were directing water onto the flames. We could see figures still going into the wide front door and figures coming out with items, the dark pictures of the early Briscoes, and Joe and Virg Sugrue with armfuls of documents, and Lana Jane Sugrue carrying those little German statues that the lawyer Briscoe loved as being mementoes of his marriage. I propped myself against Thomas and gazed. John Cole braked the wagon and leaped down to go to their assistance. Minutes later I saw him go into the house and minutes later come back out, carrying the canopy of the lawyer Briscoe's bed. The base and mattress soon followed in the care of other men. Then it was that old shiny table he worked at and then it was big brasses from the kitchen and whatever else anyone could grab. The men with the water hose slaved at the work. I saw a long long snake cross the road in front of us, going down into the little creek. I knew this big engine was pulling the water from there. Desperate miracles.

The lawyer Briscoe himself emerged, all black of face, waving his book of roses. He was calling out in a state of hectic calm. To set the lawyer Briscoe's house alight. That was a terrible venture. Now John Cole clambered back on the wagon, maybe mindful of me.

'What Jesus name going on?' said Thomas.

'Petrie's boys, they done fired the house. Came out of the woods and fired it. Were in their burlap sacks and all. Why they wear those hoods? Ain't that how everyone know them? Crazy boys. Shot the horses in the stable so they couldn't ride for help. The lawyer Briscoe and Joe and Virgil saw them off. Then Joe Sugrue raced across country in the black darkness and roused the firemen. Else the house was lost for sure.'

'We best kick on,' said Thomas, looking at me. 'This girl faint as the moon.'

'I all right,' I said.

'That fever talking maybe,' he said. 'You look like Death's sister.'

So John Cole shook the reins at the horses. My mule had a horror of the flames and was bucking and snorting at the back.

'You go on, you go on,' said Thomas.

Just as he spoke and in spite of the great flower of

water from the hose I saw the flames enrichen in the lower floor. I thought of the office there with that familiar silence now being burst through by fire. The flames widened and broke the glass of windows in an enthusiasm to be out into the night air. The tin-hatted boys, the lawyer Briscoe, Lana Jane and her brothers, all seemed to draw back in the same attitude, and hands went to heads in shocked despair. Then with a moon-high explosion the flames ignored all beams and floors or scorched them so heartily they were gone, and with a shocking eruption took up residence in the roof, and there raged and ranted, till they blossomed out through the shingles and victoriously whooshed up into the sky of old stars, making fools of rafters and petals of those mere slates.

O

Not for the first time my kind friend Rosalee Bouguereau carried me into the cabin. There was no trace of the Spencer rifle in the holster because I begged her to check before ever she took me in her arms. She said, no, child, it ain't there. She didn't fuss about it. Oh, but it grieved me to hear her words. How would I face Tennyson? When he did come in to see me, he was as bright as a sunbeam. He stroked my face and pointed at my wound and shook his head. He was both happy and angry in the same breath. He didn't ask about the Spencer. Well, he couldn't speak, but there are ways to ask other than in words. Maybe he knew from Rosalee. I swore to myself in secret that I would find him another, somehow, or search the four compass points of Tennessee to find it, if I did nothing else in my life.

Rosalee carried me in then and took off the yellow dress and asked me where I had got it but I couldn't style an answer. I didn't know how to frame that story. The wound had bled again from the journey so that the dress was now rightly stained, three or four times over, and indeed the dried blood had stiffened and blackened the cotton. She asked me where the trews were and the shirt but again I couldn't ferret up an answer. I could not be lying to Rosalee Bouguereau. I was more wretched about the rifle than the wound. She spread a mess of straw on the ground and set herself to sleep there. Soon the cabin was heavy with night and I heard the famous snoring of John Cole through the walls and I thought of the lawyer Briscoe's fine house burning and my eyes were being stolen by sleep.

'That a nice little linsey, I clean that nice for you,' Rosalee said, from the floor.

'I thank you,' I said. 'I thank you, Rosalee.'

O

Quickly enough due to Dr Tharpe's ministrations the wound closed and healed.

Tennyson Bouguereau continued to show no bitterness about the gun. He was sparing me. Well I knew it.

The biggest story in the cabin was the firing of the lawyer Briscoe's house, and why that had happened, and what might happen next. John Cole was of the opinion that men like Zach Petrie and Aurelius Littlefair knew the ground had improved under their rebel feet. When Lige Magan went into Paris for provisions it was all the talk there too. That and the colonel's chaotic raid. In the store of Mr Scruggs which now had the benefit of our patronage, Lige sensed a wariness to speak too openly but also he could read the fear writ on faces plain enough.

His worry then was that Zach Petrie might come out our way finally to avenge his brother's death, or punish us for Tennyson and Colonel Purton, or whatever he imagined were the imperatives of the war against his enemies. John Cole was as jumpy as a jackrabbit and put us all to picket duty, and one by one we relieved each other, just like proper soldiers. Lige Magan brought the old bell in from the barn that used to toll the slaves in from the fields, and that he hooked up as a warning to be sounded, especially by good wordless Tennyson. In the meantime he was pulling on with the crop but we were coming into that time where the sun deepened and hotted up and his main task with the tobacco and the corn was to hoe the devil weeds out of the fields.

Word out from the town was that Colonel Purton lost three men at West Sandy Creek and although I thought I had seen bodies lying around the houses there, no one seemed to believe that any of Zach Petrie's fifty souls was killed. Lige Magan said that Purton's lead had sunk in the gauge. If you were going to go killing rebels, well, you had best have a tally for it. But that had not happened, though I knew they had been surprised by the attack and hadn't even had time to put on their trews let alone the burlap sacks they liked to wear to keep their faces unknown. Maybe the time was coming for them to be known and return as strange heroes and that was what troubled Lige Magan's sleep, and troubled us all.

As for my part in the advancement against Zach Petrie's city, I was instructed by Thomas and John never to attempt such a folly again and by God if I did they didn't know what they might need to do and furthermore they were grateful if not to God then the devil that I had come back safe. Then there was the topic of Jas Jonski. I had been brought to him, right enough, in an error of judgement by the man who had recognised me as his fiancée, but if that wasn't a signal to ride out hightail for Lige's and deliver the news, they didn't know what was. And only for Memucan Tharpe they might never have known where I was, not for days and days, by which time, Thomas McNulty said, he would have been ready for Old Blockley. And all through this sort of talk was that under-song of despair that oftentimes attends the conversation of parents when it comes to their children's actions. This I knew and I laboured to reassure them as you might reassure children troubled by phantoms and vexing thoughts.

John Cole was of a strong mind to go into Paris and have words with Jas Jonski and maybe even, he said, just lose his head and bedamned to it and thrash that boy with a willow stick. I didn't beg him not to and I didn't beg him to. I was so confounded and confused by Jas Jonski that I had no words in English or Lakota to cover him. He was a closed book and the book was athwart with iron. Sometimes I was troubled by a good thought for him that rose unbidden. It was just a last spark of what I had felt for him in the past but it troubled me. Sometimes we are so foolish in our thoughts that even fools would baulk at what we are thinking.

Maybe part of my medicine was to be thinking about the Spencer rifle. I tried to think back to the journey through the woods and fields and at what point maybe the Spencer was last noticed by me and since that bear had set the mule to rearing was there a possibility that the gun had gone clattering away then and so if I returned to the spot would I find it? So then I was plotting as a person does to think of a way to go back there without the roars and worry of John Cole and without driving poor Thomas to Old Blockley Asylum, as he had attested might happen.

No part of me wished to be in a dress and I held fast to boy's garb and Thomas was so kind as to throw me his second-best pair of old army trews and these in fact had a very agreeable yellow stripe down the leg because they were proper cavalry trousers that used to give the cavalrymen the nickname of yellowlegs before the war. They were the trousers he had had assigned to him on his first engagement in the army many years before when as he told me he and John Cole were sent riding into California to do something about the Yuroks. That something was not told so much as seemed a gaping hollow in his mouth to tell and a fiery terror in his eyes. Whitemen don't have good history, they only have black stories they wish were otherwise.

Just neighbour to thoughts of Tennyson's lost gun was that girl Peg and the yellow dress. As good as her word Rosalee washed out the bloodstain twenty times and then worked up the basin into a great foam of suds and struck that dress with a wooden paddle and then she drew it through the little creek a thousand times and then when she was satisfied with her work so far she crushed up some dried toadstools she favoured for yellow and put the yellow back into the linsey. She dried it all out in the new sun of summer and I don't know if it wasn't as good as new and could have been craved by a princess.

But I wasn't going to wear it and anyhow it belonged to Peg. I couldn't imagine her making a visit to me polite or otherwise so in my deepest heart I reckoned I had to go to her. That, when first thought by me, seemed a rightly crazy and a reckless thought but many crazy and reckless thoughts become less so by thinking them a few times.

Rosalee was not entirely happy about the dress since she had worked so hard to make good of it and she didn't think yellowleg trews were a fit fashion for a girl but on giving up this belief she to her credit asked Lige Magan to purchase five and one half yards of osnaburg so she could make a pair of summer trews for me and it wasn't very long before she measured me for this and carried out her plan. After the war free clothes used to come down to Paris from Boston to be given in charity to the new freedmen but Rosalee like indeed an Indian person wouldn't countenance the wearing of clothes once worn by unknown strangers. They were only for burning. But none of that mattered because she was a highly expert seamstress and when the moths attacked Thomas McNulty's two dresses in his bedroom it seemed to be just the work of a day to her to put them right again though one of them was a stage dress from Grand Rapids with proper Massachusetts lace. That was the one time I saw Rosalee embraced by Thomas McNulty but whether he found a speech for his emotion might be doubted.

Otherwise we felt that strange sense of aftermath that follows disaster which has always its own promise of disaster renewed bubbling through it. So that when nothing came, no riders rode out against us, we began foolishly to feel almost a disappointment, when of course we should have been feeling a jubilant relief.

Then, since we appeared to be in a period of unexpected marvels, Jas Jonski rode out to us to 'explain himself'. I must tell you this following part with a steadiness I didn't feel at that time and maybe still don't.

O

I am sure if we had a lively sense of our danger Jas Jonski did too of his own, for his own reasons.

What did I think about Jas Jonski? I thought now he was the one that hurt me as only a man can hurt a woman – break into her like a murderous thief and bring a killing insult to her heart. I took Peg as the attorney for the matter. I had told her the story and she had opined. Why should a girl as lost as me be given that great authority?

I did not know. But I had taken the measure of Frank Parkman and somehow couldn't account him.

I had no other suspects that I knew of. Whiskey had drowned the memory but the soul of the memory lived on in me. It beat inside me.

As so much time had gone by I was beginning to be horrified by a sense that what had happened to me was a nothing, a nothing served upon a nothing. It was a strange potent thought that wormed into me, that went to the nest of my best thoughts and started to rampage there. That thought weighed down on me to crush me. I thought while in the grip of it that even if I spoke clearly now and said to the men what I thought Jas Jonski had done I would be surprised and mazed by their answer. That they would sit there nonplussed and unbeguiled and wonder why I had taken the matter so to heart. A small little thing of no account that all girls had to bear in the general affairs of the world. That it would mean nothing to them and that the word nothing would be much in their mouths as they applied it to me. Under this thought I perished time and time again. I shivered in my sense of dreadful smallness. I heard them laughing at me and looking at each other in mocking amaze and then I imagined them turning from me and never speaking to me again in the same deep loving manner for which I held them famous in my heart. That they would consider me defiled as the preachers might say and that not even Rosalee could sew me good again and that not even a spring and summer could redeem that filthy winter. That now I would be a bargain of no price and just a slave's linsey of no value and now the whippoorwill would never sound for me again nor would Thomas McNulty show me his motherly kindness nor John Cole his fatherly concern. That they might want then to deposit me on the road as a Confederate dollar of no worth to be picked up by any wanderer, that I was to be a thing discarded and no one ever sent for my retrieval. That in breaking the tiny door into myself Jas Jonski had left the house of myself ever open to the winds, to the howls of the storms, and the ransack of any passing marauder.

Chapter Thirteen

Thus occurred one of the strangest conversations I was ever witness to. It had more darkness in it than any daylight could unpick.

It is fair to say that Jas Jonski showed courage coming out there to Lige's where he had no friend he knew of. Where he was obliged to stand in front of four hostile men and two glowering women and not even an invitation. Far from it. More like six souls happy to have his hide on a door. He came as he had the first time – that is, the first time he came to plead his case, not the days of his many visitations as a suitor. I suppose I thought the mystery of Tennyson's attackers had been solved in the person of Aurelius Littlefair and his companions. But had Wynkle King taken his cue from Jas Jonski's story of woe, beyond the ken even of the colonel?

It seemed to me life was a mire when you had so much said and so much not said and in between the two all the things that could have only been said by angels – who are supposed to know everything.

That was the little platoon against him, the four

men and Rosalee and myself. It was a bright summer's evening. He had been seen coming from a long way off, north-east of the cabin. Rosalee had been on picket just that hour. The men had been eating stew inside and now had come forth at her bidding to meet this red-faced boy.

He was a man on a mission, but he still had awful trouble with his mare's head, trying to tie her to a stump post as before.

'Goddamn it,' he said.

He had twelve eyes watching him without a word or a greeting of any kind.

First duty he must have reckoned he had, he walked right up to Tennyson and held out his hand.

'I just sorry you took those blows,' he said. 'I don't mean you no harm, Mr Bouguereau.'

Tennyson didn't hold out his hand, but it might have been confusion as much as caution or unfriendliness.

'Just reckon I should be saying so,' said Jas Jonski. 'Just reckon.'

Then he stepped back again about five paces off the men. At this point I came down from the porch and walked right up beside John Cole and more or less planted myself in the earth and maybe I would show a crop later.

'I just want to say in addition to my previous speech that Winona was brought in to me in great trouble from her wound. I never fetched her nor nothing. It was Wynkle King found her on the road and ferried her to my lodgings.'

I thought, that was not what he told Dr Tharpe. Didn't he say the colonel's men coming back from the fight found me? He did. And Wynkle King hadn't known me from Adam. I said nothing for the moment, respecting his air of Socrates before the five hundred farmers.

'I never had no chance to go tell you about it and anyhow Memucan Tharpe he done it just as good,' he said, going on with his peroration despite my thoughts, as you might say. 'And I called him in and he got two dollars off me for the privilege of doctoring Winona. And I was full glad to do it. I just saying, I ain't no taker of girls and I ain't no nothing except the man that wants to marry her.'

I remember only a sort of Hmm sound out of John Cole, which may or may not have been disapproval or disbelief.

'You think you still fixing to marry her?' said Rosalee behind us, maybe mostly to herself. 'You a brainless fool.'

Jas Jonski was so worked up with his speeches and very likely so clear terrified of John Cole and the others standing there that I have to report he started to cry. He just broke out into sobs like a child and I don't suppose he was glad to be doing so. But tears will rise unbidden. Well I knew it.

'You ain't got no business here except with me,' I said.

I asked my men to go back up on the porch so I could be alone to talk to this boy. They didn't mind doing that since in truth they were right there as armed as emperors. But I suddenly saw the use in talking to him when I was covered by their strength. At the same time I prayed backwards in time to my mother for my own strength. I knew a great wound had been done to me and the truth was I could feel something at the centre of me starting to rot away, that was how it seemed to me, and it frightened me greatly. You have to try to shore up the levee when the flood races down. Even with your bare hands.

'Winona,' he said, 'I ain't a farmboy or a fool. I know you cross with me. I ain't just such a great fool. When you come in carried by Wynkle King I thought I just die to see you. Bullet wound in my girl.'

'I just ain't your girl,' I said.

'I come out here before and I say I don't know how that previous injury happen you and that still the God's truth. I lie in that bed of mine at night and I wonder how it will all be fixed. I got my mother and she turns out the biggest Indian hater I ever met in my whole life. She saying, oh, it good James that you don't go marrying no Injun, and I know such and such a girl in Knoxville, and I going to bring you there to see her, and I say, Mamma, I ain't going marrying no Knoxville girl I go marrying only Winona Cole. You ain't going to go marrying no Injun, she cries.'

'Well, you ain't,' I said. 'She right.'

'What happen that time you got the cuts and blows? Winona, what happen that time?'

So I stopped talking so quick then. I was thinking. I was trying to remember. It was like trying to bust a light of a lamp through dark fog. It can't be done.

'I just say I got a foggy head about it,' he said, also mentioning fog. 'Yes, I say to Lige Magan, I say, Lige, I don't know what happened, I as much in the dark as you all – but is that true? I been trying, trying to think. Now, I know it was – it was wrong to give you whiskey, tarnation I see it was, and it was wrong to drink whiskey myself, since I don't even like it, and I never do drink it, but we was drinking it – do you remember being up in the hayloft at Frank's? I kinda remember that. I don't even like to not remember. I remember how sweet and kind you were, and we were kissing . . .'

'No, I don't remember. And I don't believe I ever was in no hayloft at Frank Parkman's place of employment.'

'You was. And I was. I do remember that.'

The men and Rosalee stirred on the porch when Jas Jonski raised his voice. He saw that straight off and kept it low again.

'I swear to the Lord you were there, you were there,

you and me, and we were laughing, and kissing, and then I swear to the same good Lord, I have no recollection, none at all, at what happen next.'

'I can tell you, and Rosalee Bouguereau could tell you if she weren't so shy. When I came home with bruises, and cuts to my face, and my heart failing in my breast from fear, and no memory of nothing, I had blood, you know, *there*, and Jas, I was torn, and someone done did that, and I say it was you, because who else in the world would do that, excepting someone I was let kiss me. Another man tries to kiss me and he not my sweetheart, I fetch up my knife and stick it in his belly.'

Now my voice had risen high. So I was obliged to tamp it down.

'You saying someone – hurt you, there?' he said.

'I saying. That the whole nature of this import. Blackstone, chapter sixteen. It a felony, Jas Jonski – except, of course, the law don't apply to me. I ain't no citizen. Your mother right, you can't be going to go marrying no Injun, because we ain't even people. We ain't even human people. We animals, that you can beat and harry and hurt as you please.'

I hadn't raised my voice for that. I hadn't needed to. I never saw a boy's face blanch so. He was already a whiteman, now he was an even whiter whiteman.

'You saying . . . that someone – ?'

'Yes, Jas Jonski, yes, I saying – why you thinking we been all through this mire of trouble?'

'I thought some black-hearted fool maybe striked you down, or your mule throwed you, or I don't know – but never that, not one second I had of thinking that.'

'You is just a God's fool, Jas Jonski, because what I saying is what happen most often all the time. You likely thinking all those brave soldiers out at the wars was bringing soup to Indians? And Thomas McNulty and Lige and John Cole all dainty dancing across the plains?'

'They know you were hurt like that?' he said.

'No, they don't know because I don't tell them. If I tell them, Jas, they kill you. They kill you till you be dead. You know why? Because they love me as a daughter. But Rosalee know, because she had to take her cloth and wipe away the blood.'

Jas Jonski didn't talk then, he was standing there with all these words going into his head and then he was trying to sort them into places where he could regiment them.

'And you reckon it was me, that I did that?' he said finally.

'Who else?'

'You reckon that maybe I done that and then I hit you and broke your face?'

'I guess.'

'You might think I'd have a memory of that,' he said, in a small sweating voice. Maybe, I was thinking, he was an honest soul enough. He looked so affrighted. Starling Carlton took Indian children to give to whitefolk for their pleasure. Even at six I saw soldiers, I think I did, it was nothing to hurt an Indian woman or a girl – or a boy too. It was nothing. It was something the soldiers did. Oh but, Jas Jonski didn't think so. No. Just for a moment my heart went out to him and then I snatched it back, I had to.

'I understand it now,' he said. 'I just didn't have no understanding. Now I have it. Do it mean something good that I don't remember? That you don't remember? I don't believe so. I thinking I done something black and dark. In whiskey be living demons. Why I take that whiskey? I don't even crave it.'

Then he tipped his hat to the faces on the porch.

'I best be going,' he said. 'I so heartily sorry, Winona, I am. Yes, I find I am. You tell those men now what you told me and I will expect them to come for me. I would do just the same. My mother don't understand the world. The world ain't worth nothing unless you true in it. I sorry, I am.'

Then he swung himself back up on his twisty horse and rode away.

I walked back to the cabin.

'We hear wedding bells?' said Lige Magan.

'No,' I said.

'You be quiet now,' said John Cole to Lige.

'I just thinking they was talking good enough,' said Lige, abashed at his foolishness.

'Lige Magan, I never said a word in anger to you but I punch your face real good if you ain't hushing now,' said John Cole.

O

I wept all the night, holding on to Rosalee like the wheel of a little ship, but knew not why – not so I could say.

Chapter Fourteen

A person may weep all the night and sleep in the first hours of daybreak and be surprised to wake then with a tincture of rest. I did wake so. Maybe it was also true that I felt less scorned, less wounded, than I had, because there had been something in Jas Jonski's talk the day before that had comforted me, even if it was the comfort of a bad man. I looked back and forth among what I remembered of Jas Jonski's words and wondered at some of it anew and didn't know what to make of it at all. Maybe as something else to hold on to, I remembered something he had said, itself a shadowy remark. It was that Wynkle King after finding me on the road had brought me to Jas in my extremity. If that was so then might Wynkle King not know where the Spencer rifle was?

I was of a mind to find out.

I dressed in my new summer trews and for good measure a loose work shirt that Rosalee had also sewn for me. There was something in the lovely cleanliness of the Irish cloth and the neat stitching that made me feel cleaner. Made me feel dapper, and my pride rose out of that. That there could be beauty in something so poor – fifty cents for seven yards.

I found Lige Magan in the yards hitching up the wagon with Tennyson.

'Good morning to you,' said Lige. 'I sorry for making a fool of myself yesterday. Wedding bells indeed.'

'Where you fixing to go?' I said.

'Help our good friend the lawyer Briscoe – in his hour of need.'

'You bring me along?'

'You'll come back black,' he said, scanning over my new outfit.

'That don't make no odds,' I said.

'You go and fetch yourself a hat, I don't want you raving in the sun.'

The hats lived on hooks in a tiny back room and as I went through the deep shadow of the cabin I had to pass Tennyson's narrow quarters. I knew he was outside so I peeked in, like a thief. It was just an iron bed and a chair and a small table and what Rosalee called a 'person', which was three lengths of wood raised in a pyramid to hold your clothes. So that it seemed like Tennyson without Tennyson stood perpetually in the room. I never did ask him where he got the fifty dollars he must have paid for his rifle but looking at his possessions, or the lack of them, it did make me wonder. If you can own nothing, he owned it.

But every inch of the walls was covered in his drawings. Pictures of us, like you might see in a sheriff's office, but without the Wanted, and the likely reward for catching us. It was strange to see us all there. Made me pause and gaze. A stately drawing of Rosalee took pride of place.

The newest work was all of one thing – jackrabbits. Now why was that, I thought? There were maybe twenty drawings of those jackrabbits. That was strange too because a jackrabbit was just a soul to be shot at since it liked so well to eat the crops. The jackrabbit's like an orphan the minute it is born. Off it goes and it never looks back. It doesn't need a mamma. So they say. But Tennyson must have held a high opinion of that animal. Well he must have been out in the fields drawing them because here was a jackrabbit gazing this-and-that-a-way and here was a jackrabbit running like the devil's servant. Some of the drawings were splashed with the red colour he was able to make from berries. I didn't know if that was meant to signify the sunset, or maybe a killing. In truth Rosalee was a demon for that jugged-hare dish she made.

She cooked the creature whole and when you lifted the lid it was like a little person in its coffin.

I was so caught up in the drawings that I went back out without fetching a hat and was told by Lige to go right back in and rectify that.

O

My heart would have wept for the lawyer Briscoe except he was so high up in his spirits you could only wonder at him.

'Why,' he said, 'I ain't going to let no foul banditti push me under.'

He was amazed that Zach Petrie had sent men to burn his house. He had never had a crazy thought like that. Only a fool attacks the law direct and Zach Petrie was no fool. The lawyer Briscoe said what makes a criminal of a man is just one thing. Choosing, *choosing*, to do the wrong thing. See the right thing, but choose the wrong. The beams were still smouldering on his prized house but already he had called in the carpenters and the masons and by the good Lord Jesus he was going to raise the place again, he said – *instanter*, as he liked to say, momently, *cito*. Then he was quoting the Roman writer Ovid and I remember this because he had it pinned up on the wall behind his desk – till the fire took it no doubt. *Video meliora proboque, deteriora sequor.* When the lawyer Briscoe spoke Latin you knew he meant business.

He asked me would I be so kind as to act as his clerk of works for the building. Make a note of what was needed and get it all brought in and keep a record of all his expenditure. Lige Magan looked happy about that because he had been worried since the fire that I would have no wages coming in, and what I got was a goodly part of any ready money we had. The lawyer Briscoe had moved all his rescued chattels to the barn and he had bid Joe and Virg Sugrue set up his magnificent bed there and even as we spoke I could just see Lana Jane wielding her willow broom inside the soft browns of the shadows of the great building. A barn is just a giant box for dust but she was making a resolute start.

So then I was talking to the carpenters and the masons and they explained to me what they might need to make a start and the carpenters said the big timber they would need for the floors and roof would best be got from East Tennessee in the mountains where the timber was still high and plentiful. And that would need to be brought along the roads and rivers as much as possible because there was no train on God's earth could take timber that size. It surprised me how anxious they were to talk to me and even the way they stood there before me, just as gentle and friendly as you please. I held a big ledger along my left arm and was writing in it from an inkpot that Mr Otter the plasterer held for me. Although my wound was healed I was still protecting it, as people do. Mr Otter had come out of respect for the lawyer Briscoe even though plastering would not start for a long long time, he hoped in the fall when the walls were ready for him. Mr Otter didn't look like an otter so much as a heron because he had a staring eye and a beaky nose.

I was just beginning to warm to the work when I remembered why I had stolen a lift from Lige Magan. The fact was I was intent on finding out where Wynkle King had his house and I was hoping it was nearby in Paris somewhere. I could almost have asked Jas Jonski but maybe I wasn't *that* content with him. No. I supposed by Sheriff Flynn's account of him I might have discovered him in Zollicoffer's saloon but I wasn't too desirous of going there in particular if he was in his cups. I knew it was dangerous that he was in league with Zach Petrie – especially standing there before the smoking ruins of the lawyer Briscoe's house. But I had to try and find out where Tennyson's gun might be. That rifle was his fortune in life and I had lost it like a blamed fool. If Wynkle King had his quarters out at Zach Petrie's I would have to think again. But I had the notion in my head he was situated in Paris – you wouldn't come all the way from West Sandy Creek to go drinking and then be drunk on your horse and likely eaten by a mountain lion or a bear on the way back.

If I thought it was going to be a big mystery I was mistaken because when I asked Mr Otter just like that if he knew where a Wynkle King lived, he said, why, yes, he had rooms on Blythe Street above the shop where Mr

Otter got his horsehair. Mr Otter said he made his own lath out of greenwood but he was damned if he was going to go shaving a horse. So that was surprising. This Wynkle King seemed very well known for a youngster.

So when I was done for that morning with my business for the lawyer Briscoe I told Lige Magan I would come back towards evening because I was going to go walking into the town. Lige Magan had shifted himself with a shovel and was shovelling the ashes and the burnt ruins with twenty other men, and twenty more were bringing barrows back and forth from where they had chosen to dump the debris. They were going to clear everything and then see what could be saved and what could not. For instance the lawyer Briscoe had high hopes for his stairway, which was now blackened and teetering but all the same more or less itself. And maybe the two stone stacks of the chimneys and certainly he thought the old porch and verandah would rise again like phoenixes because they were made of cast-iron metal in Philadelphia – you could see that written on them here and there. But I left all those important considerations and took myself along the way into town. It was a warm day but cool enough still in that early part of the year and a little breeze touched my shirt as if it was checking Rosalee's stitching. You could sense the woods stirring with birds and all the wide and secret kingdom of those animals that don't like to be seen by man in their daily goings about. I thought of my bear going about there and whether she was able to think of me and I hoped maybe she had given me something of herself in exchange for nearly frightening me to death. Then I wondered how much of me now was still Lakota and I also wondered how my people were faring way out on the plains if they were still there having heard news of the continuing wars and knowing in my heart of hearts that the white eyes would never forgive them for their defiance. And if I didn't think that, the *Paris Invigilator* thought it for me.

And all this going about that *I* was doing, in the forest of the white eyes as you might say and not my own forest, Tennyson, Rosalee, Lige, even Thomas McNulty and John Cole, I thought all that was a story that had happened because the story that was given me at the start was never to be. Never to get going beyond a certain point and was only fated to end so close to the beginning you couldn't squeeze a straw into the gap.

If they had let my mother live and my sister and had never come into our country how would it be now? I would have no notion or word of English and I would believe that the most important people in the world were ourselves and that there would be found on the earth no one to match us for goodness and majesty. And I thought I would have to be doing all the chores of the camp unless I was like my mother and would be allowed to be a fighter. I might have been a woman fighter for my people and have had great fame among them like my mother.

So then that run of thinking reminded me of Tennyson's rifle.

Maybe Blythe Street was a good place to buy horsehair for a plasterer but it had the cold bare look of poor folk's houses and the road all pitted from the winter rains. My hair had grown out a little so I tucked what there was under my hat. Then I let it fall out again because I had the thought that Wynkle King had found me as a girl in a yellow dress. So I wasn't so sure of my errand then. I had a look at myself in the window of an empty shop. A shadowy little soul right enough. Strange how a body has all those high thoughts from dawn till dusk and yet might look like I looked. You wouldn't know what I was, apart from being a Lakota. A waif, like in a story. I nodded to myself to see if that was any improvement. It was suddenly surprising to me that the carpenters and the masons had even talked to me. I didn't look like a clerk of works although I had no idea what that should look like. I thought I looked like a girl in a boy's trews and shirt. Why would a girl wear those? And yet I had walked through six or seven streets to reach this street right near the heart of the town and I didn't remember anyone remarking on me. Even looking at me.

But I had come that far and so I climbed the dirty stairs to the floor above the suppliers.

The door there had a little brass plate that said W. King so it wasn't going to be I was in the wrong place. I certainly felt like I was the wrong person to be there in the right place. Maybe Wynkle King had been one of the party that fired the lawyer Briscoe's house? How could we know, since they had worn those burlap sacks they favoured, with the holes cut for eyes? Either way, he was a follower of Zach Petrie. Then I thought, maybe I am crazy, maybe I would be a better candidate for Old Blockley Asylum than Thomas McNulty. Tennyson was an altered man, did he even know how to fire his rifle any more? Why was I dogging around looking for it? Sniffing with my nose for it like a hound? What was the purpose of finding that rifle? What in tarnation was I thinking, what was I doing? I stood outside the dirty door in that dirty tenement and wondered. Maybe some blow to my head as well as the wound to my centre had driven me demented. So that I might be more justly running through the streets howling in an honest way in the true manner of a proper lunatic and not showing my madness by going to talk to murdering rebels and drunken pals of Jas Jonski? W. King. As a matter of record, as the lawyer Briscoe might say, the nameplate said Rev. W. King. Rev. for reverend I supposed. But Wynkle King was a friend of Jas Jonski so I couldn't imagine he was more than twenty years of age and I didn't think reverends came so young.

I knocked on the door.

If you can be twenty years old and yet look deceased, Wynkle King fitted the bill. I had never seen him up close – maybe I had never actually seen him at all, but just had stories of him from Jas. Just knew the name but not the owner of it. It was a moment made odder by the fact that he must have lifted me off the wagon road and what – laid me across his horse? I just didn't know. And had the mule lingered near me when I fainted? He was a tender-hearted mule, I knew, so I hoped he had.

'I just looking for Wynkle King, wanted to ask him something,' I said.

'I Wynkle.'

'I would like to take this opportunity, sir, to thank you for saving my life.'

'I never saved your life,' he said, looking inclined to close the door again.

He was eyeing me up and down like he wanted to ask, why you dressed like a jackass boy?

'Didn't you find me up on the road and bring me down to Jas Jonski?'

'No.'

'That were me,' said a voice from inside the room.

'That were you?' I said. 'Who?'

I peered in. There were two windows running the front of the house so there was plenty of light.

'That were me, I guess,' said a man within. 'You was wearing a yellow dress on that occasion.'

'That right,' I said. 'So you – you ain't Wynkle King?'

'I Wynkle,' he said.

Chapter Fifteen

'He's my pa,' said the younger Wynkle with his dead face.

'Oh,' I said, nonplussed.

Then, as if he wished to attest to his bladder's fame, he left the room in a rush – I heard the tinkle of piss in some hidden receptacle – and all the while myself still puzzling.

But maybe Jas Jonski never did say which Wynkle King brought me, and maybe come to think of it Colonel Purton never said which Wynkle King was a confederate and accomplice of Zach Petrie. Both Wynkle Kings I can confirm lived in the same level of dirt and dereliction because the room lacked a woman's touch. A bear might have lived cleaner in it.

'How you know to bring me to Jas Jonski?' I said, before I could think better of it.

'You told me, you darn fool,' said the reverend.

'I told you? I don't remember.'

'You said it, *Jas Jonski, Jas Jonski*, you said, and I said to myself, that's Wynkle's good friend works at Mr Hicks's. So. I obliged you. You were in a bad way, missy.'

The younger Wynkle came sheepishly back, blushing as red as a fall apple.

'Was my mule nearby on the road?' I said.

'He was.'

'Was there a Spencer rifle in a holster?'

'There was.'

'And do you mind if I ask you where it might be now?'

'I took it for taxes.'

'You took Tennyson's rifle? Ain't you a reverend?'

'You meaning Tennyson Bouguereau, that likely shot Tach Petrie?'

'He didn't shoot Tach Petrie.'

'How you know?'

'Because I was there.'

'So you shot him maybe?' He laughed at my silence. 'If I had known you were connected I wouldn't have carried you to Jas Jonski, no, sir.'

Oh, this was not going good – or in any direction I had hoped. First there were two Wynkles, which was awkward enough. But also the reverend had leaped on Tennyson's name. And if Aurelius Littlefair had struck down Tennyson – which he had, according to this very witness – whether because he knew about Jas Jonski's embarrassment, or just to settle an old score while he had him handy, or just because he was a freedman, well, here was a bosom pal of Aurelius Littlefair. I felt the danger of that powerfully. Had I really expected to walk up to this door and be given the rifle with a thank you and farewell? Looked like I had. Especially when I had thought it was just a weedy boy involved.

'Give me that gun,' I cried.

He laughed again: 'It ain't here, missy. I sold it. To Zach. I sell everything.'

And he indicated with an opening gesture of his right hand and a dipping turn of his head the utter emptiness of the room.

The younger Wynkle looked from his father to me, and from me to his father.

'What you want me to do, Pa?'

'Just seize her, son,' said the reverend.

Oh, but, you need to be quick to grab Winona Cole. I leaped back from the door and just about slithered down the stairs. If my feet touched them I didn't feel it. I ran out into the street and kept running. I didn't know which Wynkle King was a slave to beer, as the colonel had said, but thought maybe it must darn well be both of them because neither came galloping after me. But I ran till the end of my breath just in case.

O

The lawyer Briscoe's Blackstone said it wasn't a crime to retrieve something stolen from you just so long as you didn't break a law getting it back. I would have been happy to break a law getting the rifle back from that scrawny pair of Wynkles – happy to shoot them – happy to skin them. Except maybe he had done me a good turn, the reverend, in his state of innocence. But he didn't look like he was shaping to do me another good turn any time soon. Question was, as I tramped back to the lawyer Briscoe's site of catastrophe, where was the rifle? Had I been standing near it? Was I going to have to sneak back some dark night when hopefully father and son might be downing whiskey in Zollicoffer's? I shuddered at the peril of that. My mind could easily show me the going wrong of it. I almost felt the damp hands of the reverend seizing me.

Of course he had said he had sold it to Zach Petrie.

Going home in the cart with Lige Magan I thought I had best tell him about Wynkle King.

'Everyone know the reverend,' said Lige. 'He a lying lowdown thieving braggart. A poultice of a man. You lucky he didn't cook you.'

'Cook me?' I said.

'That why they took the collar off of him. Why, it is said he dined off his enemies. He were a chaplain at the Injun Wars. Now you can do a lot of things in the army as I know but you can't eat an Indian.'

'Lige.'

'Yep, took a young girl and ate her. Cooked her good first. With some nice herbs. Did ten years for that.'

'Lige Magan, you teasing your own friend's daughter?'

'Well, I – maybe just a little bit.'

'Lige?'

'Yep?'

'Fact is I done lost Tennyson's rifle and I want so bad to get it back. I seeing myself go in to him with it in my arms and his face lighting up with joy to see it.'

'Winona, that poor man don't have such a lighting in him now,' said Lige, shaking his head.

'Ain't he?'

'No, he don't know Tuesday from Tallahassee.'

My right arm clenched of its own volition and my hand tamped down into a vigorous fist. I almost thought my wound would open in my shoulder such was the force of it. It was a gesture that wanted vengeance on those that had so inconvenienced Tennyson in his admirable life.

'Colonel Purton ain't done yet, no, he ain't,' said Lige Magan. 'He made a brave assault upon those desperate men. While you were gone he came talking. Says he lost three men but took down seven of theirs – even if a woman was among their number. Anyway, rebel women just as murder-minded as men, I notice. I do notice that.

Well, I see your regard for Tennyson, and I share it. Always said if he went before I would bury his rifle in with him as a keepsake for the next world.'

Like he might need it in heaven for hunting but what would you hunt in heaven?

'He still drawing his drawings good, I seen them,' I said, as much to calm myself as anything.

'Maybe so, but he don't know Tuesday from Tallahassee.'

'I still like to get that rifle back. Ain't there fifty dollars in that gun?'

'I expect. But he never paid no fifty dollars for it.'

'No?'

'No, my father the late lamented Luther Magan, he gave it to him when the war ended. Said he was going to need it. I guess he was right. Right about most things.'

'I guess he was your good old pa?' I said, spotting this small door in Lige for a sentimental moment and desirous of entering there for a reason that was obscure to me. Otherwise he was as hard as flintstone all the while. But fact was we *loved* Lige Magan. And I liked to see him sentimental if only the one rare time in his life.

'My pa?' he asked, though it seemed to me it was not a question to me but to himself. I waited to hear his answer, but he didn't say anything else.

O

Now we had come up to Whit Monday and that was a day that Lige Magan gave as a holiday. No soul was to stoop to work that day. Lige set his Rotary firewater on the table for any to drink that wished.

Thomas McNulty was accustomed on Pentecost eve to kill a suckling pig and hang it and allow it slowly to bleed its blood into a bucket. Then on the holy Monday up stepped the wizard Rosalee and made her blood pudding. And Lige lit the wood fire in the yard and ran a long iron spike through the pig and then he stood there like a sentry turning the spit.

Like a picket against the burning of the meat.

This was a joyous day even for those that didn't have joy inside them. A mortgaged joy that even mournful folk could borrow. Then you saw Lige Magan risen with his fiddle and the lovely calm close of that summer day. And the wood saved from the woods all round burning brightly, and its first shadows like children leaping in the yard. It was the day for beginning all again and though it was in the aftertime of Leavenworth when he was seldom in his dress, Thomas McNulty on Whit Monday donned his dress. Because the thing that Rosalee most craved to see was the old dance he used to dance in Grand Rapids when he was so handsome and beautiful that hard miners asked for his hand.

Which was a thing I saw for myself. They would come like a gaggle to the stage door, looking for the beautiful woman that had beguiled them so. And Thomas going out past them not even glanced at, in the man's attire he put on to walk home in, a smile on his lips.

Now in his age he could never be so fancied but there with his friends and the man who so loved him we revered him. We watched his lonesome dance. His feet were still small in his patent shoes and the metal beads on the dress still threw light onto his painted face. John Cole was stood at the window while the night fell all around him. Years fell away and maybe to himself he was young again and Thomas was young and they were in their heyday of hope and enterprise.

The pig was eaten with solemn joy and Rosalee sang an old song in a lingo she herself didn't know but had earnestly learned at her grandmother's knee. Oh, stately Rosalee. And if Tennyson's part was no longer his fabled singing, still and all there was something of a song in the way he watched his sister. And when Lige had pulled a few glasses from his whiskey, then the fiddle was let free. And I shook my sorrows from myself and showed what I knew of the world in a wild Lakota dance. And it was all freedom, that Pentecostal Monday, when love was palpable between us. And the way that John Cole touched Thomas's back as the two of them stood watching in the long shadows of May.

❍

Well, the lawyer Briscoe if anything he seemed to be granted new life by the catastrophe. Maybe he relished a tide he could push against. Anyway, he said, this recent madness was likely the knife to lance the boil. He meant the mad boil of hatreds then current in Henry County. He was a buoyant optimist when other folk were sinking stones, certainly. Joy over despair. It was a tactic of war and courage, like not crying out when your enemy tortures you. Among the Lakota there was a society for young men which obliged them to say everything in its opposite meaning. If they wanted to say *I love thee*, they said *I hate thee*. They even walked backwards. They tied their headdress feathers to their ankles. It was a kind of magic and the lawyer Briscoe practised his version of it. He had saved his bed, his bible and his book of roses and he was ready to start again. That was how it seemed.

A man deserted by his grand wife and never having sight of his children maybe has learned something at the hem of misfortune.

I marked my sheets and orders were sent out in every direction. A clerk of works is a harried soul. A house was a huge web of numbers and I marvelled at the true army that had to be mustered to raise it back into the sky. Numbers for this, numbers for that.

Judah Mundy the little foreman struggled against the workmen who were not inclined to work. That made him swell with anger. Like a dead sheep in the sun on the side of the road. He planted his boots in front of men twice his size, spitting venom in their faces – or at least in the direction of their faces. They gasped at his passion.

'If you get fifty cents a day for a job you best go do it,' he said. 'Goddamn lazy sons of mountain cats.'

'Goddamn lazy sons of mountain cats,' he hissed again at the trembling white eyes. He didn't have to hiss at the freedmen, who were plumb glad of the work.

'The foreman remembers the man who works to his limit, and that is the worker's fame and fortune. No one loves that man who lurks in the woodshed shying off work, because his slack must be taken up by others.'

Such was his little homily.

In a few weeks the site was cleared of everything that spoke of Zach Petrie's inferno – the cinders, the charred spars, the thousand items buckled by heat, the tottering beams, the injured walls, the sooty furniture.

The lawyer Briscoe hesitated now and then. He gazed on the ruined body of the huge dresser in the kitchen.

'Fifty years of service,' he said in a laden voice.

Its shelves which had displayed jelly moulds and pots like thieves of light and sun-bright pans for big fishes and roasts were roasted to charcoal themselves, all the wood burned biscuit thin. Lana Jane Sugrue stood at his elbow crying softly and twisting her tiny hands as if a supplicant witness for the accused.

He weighed up the force of its history in his heart and the blackened calamity it now was and ordered it to be taken out onto the lawns. It tottered in a state of shock at its sudden exposure and was executed by axes and burned.

It was all numbers, that house building. Numbers like little songs, like little birds. A small heaven of numbers. The lawyer Briscoe made me feel somehow that things would improve and my heart would heal and we could look back with fortitude on what had befallen us – and forward to the future with the proverbial measure of hope. But then of course there was no past, present, and future, as my mother knew. There was only a hoop turning in tightly on itself, over and over. Truth lay in a hole so deep no boy could dig a well to it. So deep no mule could enter its caverns with a lanthorn on his head.

Chapter Sixteen

During this time Tennyson Bouguereau took down all the drawings in his room and made a little bonfire of them behind the cabin. His sister was distraught.

'You come and talk to this stupid man,' she said to me, 'since you the only living soul he heeds.'

'He heeds you before all, Rosalee,' I said.

'Maybe long ago, maybe long ago, but now that he is an idiot, he looks to you.'

I didn't think he was an idiot but I said nothing to that. I did like to sit with him and talk and I was sure he had understood the attack on Zach Petrie was for his sake. Well, I wasn't so right about that either.

Over the days following he began to make other drawings. Now the big jackrabbit was drawn attacking what looked like a man. Rosalee brought me in to see them all pinned about the room as before. She shook her head and was on the edge of tears.

'I think his head going to explode and then I be picking up his brains,' she said.

That evening we were resting on the porch and

Thomas McNulty was telling Lige Magan stories that Lige already knew and so relished all the more because of that – they were stories of their time in the war. I went to Tennyson where he sat alone and apart in the far shadows. I told him that when I was little in Wyoming there was always a man that drew what they called a Winter Count, which was a sort of history in pictures of what had happened to the tribe that year. I told him that the Lakota had no writing so the skill to make those pictures was very important. I asked him was there a story in his pictures of the jackrabbits and the men. Behind my words there was a certainty that this hurt man was not crazy. All I really meant to do was prove that for Rosalee and set her mind at rest.

Tennyson got up and beckoned me to follow him. He picked up a lanthorn where it hung on an ancient hook and I went with him to his room. There he shone the light on his pictures one by one and then looked at me as if he thought any fool could read what they said.

'Why is the jackrabbit attacking the man?' I said.

In answer he straightened two fingers and put them to his top lip. I was none the wiser. Then with something of the scurry of a vexed child, he went to his table and put the other hand into his store of red, and rubbed it into one side of his face. Then he put the fingers up again and then made a gesture of savage blows. When I still didn't understand he stood there like a hunting dog that had been run till it could run no further. He seemed so tired suddenly his legs could barely hold him up.

That night I lay in bed with Rosalee deep in sleep curled up against my spine. I couldn't find the thread of slumber. I was thinking and thinking about Tennyson. Then slowly I began to get drowsy, and must have been at that strange gate between sleep and waking. Suddenly I thought I understood. Jackrabbit = hare. Hare + the two fingers raised = harelip. Red paint on Tennyson's face = port-wine stain. Harelip + port-wine stain = Colonel Purton. If he meant Colonel Purton was the jackrabbit, who was the other man?

It was the small owl-ridden hours of the night but I was so stirred by these revelations and inspirations that I climbed away from Rosalee and slipped through the quiet cabin to Tennyson's room. I had no qualms about going in and waking him, I was so strangely agitated. I shook his shoulder and he awoke with a serene expression on his face. The moon was helpful with its light in the little window. He knew I was neither thief nor murderer.

'Is the jackrabbit in the drawing a man with a harelip and a red stain on his face?'

Well, he made no response at first. Maybe he was sweeping the debris of sleep off his thoughts. Then he screwed up his eyes and nodded.

'And who is the other man, Tennyson, who is that?'

Tennyson took a hand slowly out of the sheets and sacks and slowly slowly raised it and then at last pointed at his own self.

'You?' I said. 'The jackrabbit attacked you? The jackrabbit hurt you?'

And he nodded again. Then he turned over and went back to his snoring.

I returned to my own bed, pondering, wondering.

If Colonel Purton had attacked Tennyson Bouguereau, well, why did he do that? If it wasn't Aurelius Littlefair, who now lived in my thoughts as a fiery demon, then why did Sheriff Flynn say it was, or why did Wynkle King say it?

The owls in the woods behind went on with their calling. The owl when he calls fluffs out his beard like a little man. Now and then one screeched like a captive girl, and screeched again.

◑

When a Sunday came and that lie-abed Christian world was at rest I folded the yellow dress and wrapped it in an old square of paper that Rosalee had saved and tied it about with baccy twine. I didn't want to cut a new length so I used an old piece blackened by tobacco. But it was

Peg's dress, I told myself, and I had no use for it. And if I could get to Petrie's camp, I told myself, then Tennyson's Spencer might be somewhere about.

Those were the reasons I gave myself for going. The true reasons were hidden from me I do not doubt.

I guess my favourite mule had forgiven me for abandoning him because he took the saddle and bridle without complaint. Since the world is its own master the day was paying no heed to anything but its own effort to light the sky. Glimmer by growing glimmer that wide old sky of Tennessee turned soft blue. Not a cloud dared dirty it. I could feel the sunlight start to raise the hairs on my arms. The underbrush and little oaks seemed to crackle with invisible flames. There was something in the journey that made me happy. But I had no words to say what. Because in truth it was a dangerous journey, a stupid one. My mind would not let me think so. I had the parcel lashed to the pommel. It bounced there slightly like an unleavened loaf. That was my courage somehow. I thought of the yellow dress nesting in the parcel, folded, clean, and neat.

Soon I had passed the lawyer Briscoe's and gazed at the works so far for the new house all stilled and strange. Piles of timber lay under sacking in numbers I actually knew. Upturned heaps of lime and pallets of shingles. I supposed the lawyer Briscoe was asleep on his fine bed in the barn – his hill of a belly rising and falling. And somewhere nesting in new niches, Lana Jane, Virg, and Joe. I heard the chapel bells competing on the warming air in Paris to hasten the citizenry into their Sunday best.

I skirted the town and got up on the eastern road, looking for the place in the trees where I had last seen Peg.

I sneaked along, disturbing nothing in the forest and hoping the mule would take his cue from my silence. I could skirt a sleeping bear and never touch its dreams. It seemed as I went that all the incomings and changes of the whitemen passed away. Would I not be obliged to parley with the Chickasaw of the forest? They might kill me just as quick as a whiteman. Or if I was clever like my mother and could enter by the narrow doors of their friendship all would be well. Straight is the gate but once inside I would find generosity.

But the Chickasaw were only motes now in the corner of an eye.

At last I saw where my mule had tramped out those weeks ago, disturbing the ground a little, myself swaying in the saddle with my wound. This was the opening to Peg's secret way and I was intending to thread backwards along it. The little parcel with the yellow dress speaking to me without saying a word. The slight jingle of the metal in the bridle, the soft creak of the saddle under me. Such a great king of creatures is a mule. An emperor and a friend. This fellow was a devil for a thimble of molasses or a sweet apple. Lige Magan's ragged orchard gave a hundred sweet red apples which he hoarded in the apple room. An apple is a long-lived soul. I was thinking these thoughts and every few paces I was thinking, *Peg*, like the word and thought of Peg was a repeated note in an old song. All the birds of the wood were very glad of the summer – as the morning burgeoned and opened its hands, they went firing among the new leaves like the gentlest of bullets. Greens against greens, half-seen fires of feathers, a busyness and bluster that delighted me as I walked the mule along. All the while the bird-blue sky reached down to me through the branches, the soft light of the sun rested on the turns of metal and the polished leather. The mule's great ears like a crazy gunsight.

◑

Every foot of the way I was scanning the ground for Tennyson's Spencer, even though I knew it most likely was not there. But I was mindful of Lige Magan saying that Wynkle King was a black liar. I was very interested so to come into the place where the bear had demonstrated her superiority over us. I thought I could see the marks of her actions and again felt the suddenness and the strangeness of her closeness. There was no sign of the rifle.

Not more than a mile or two ahead would surely lie the camp of Zach Petrie. Would they have pickets set this time? Maybe they would be on high alert now. Someone might shoot me before ever they shouted a warning. I gathered myself into myself, trying to fold the mule also into a tiny clenched thing. I plucked out my lady's gun from my trews and held it at the ready even though such a small weapon looked ridiculous enough. Did Peg consider me a friend or an enemy? She had brought me all the way to the road, but why? Because I had saved her from drowning? Or some other reason? Because we were both Indian? Because? I knew not why. She had made no effort to see me or send a message, though I wondered if either would have been possible. Well, I was going to see her and give her the dress back. I thought again of her going about showing her bare backside in Thomas McNulty's ruined trews. I nearly laughed at the thought but then suddenly reined in the mule. Something had stirred in the leaves that wasn't a flame-coloured bird. Something had – and then as if one moment not there and the next there, Peg was on the track. She was wearing a rough brown dress and her feet were bare.

'What you doing down here in outlaw country?' she said. 'With that silly gun.'

'I—' I said.

'You lucky I not one of the sentries, girl, or you be one dead Injun now.'

'Whyever they shoot a boy on a mule before they even know his business?'

'They shoot you,' she said.

'Well, I know,' I said. 'That how it is. But, here you are instead, maybe.'

'Yep, I here, it's me. The girl you saved. The girl who shot you. How that shoulder?'

'It healed up quick and good.'

'I hear some fool carried you to the boy that hurt you?'

'I think he hurt me. I don't recall.'

'I think you do.'

'I got two items of business,' I said. 'I got your yellow dress here all cleaned of blood and my greatest desire is to fetch back that rifle you saw me with that just don't belong to me but belong to Tennyson Bouguereau.'

'You come all this way with that threadbare old dress?'

'I come to see you too, and to thank you.'

'For what?'

'For bringing me up to the road.'

'You took my hand in that bush when I was just set to drown – we square in the matter of debt. My life, your life. You had no need to come out and see me.'

'I come out to see you because – because I needed to see you, that all.'

'I never had no one *needing* to see me. Goddamn it, I never did. Maybe you fixing to kill me, maybe something in you wants to finish the work you were doing when I stopped you?'

'Well, that ain't true. Truth is, I just don't know why I came. You never do something and not be knowing why you done it?'

'Well, what is the riddle of life? To-ing and fro-ing, this-ing and that-ing, and not knowing what in tarnation we doing it all for.'

I laughed there under the lightly woven cloth of sky and trees. Suddenly I wondered, how many people were in America? Thousands and thousands. And here we were, just two of them, and one not knowing why she had ridden in there, and the other not knowing even why she breathed in and out. But something in that riddle was wanting to loose itself.

I was just gazing at her. What was I thinking, feeling? Didn't I feel and think that she was a sort of medicine? Crazy thoughts, but just the look of her? No doubt Dr Memucan Tharpe had lozenges and vials for many illnesses and maladies, so what was Peg the tincture of, what was she the cure for? I got to be honest. She was to me a sort of apparition, a sort of appearance of something. I could sense the heat in her skin under the rough cloth. I only had to reach out with just my mind to feel it. The slight length of her, the dark legs, the thin arms, the face that wanted to talk to you about the very best reason there was for this whole business of hurtful humanity going about in the world. The colours of things are not really just blues and greens and reds, there are softnesses and shadows of colours that slip away from any word to say them. That was how she was coloured. The set of her green eyes, the little slopes of her brown cheeks, the thick black hair shoved behind her ears, the lovely mouth, painted as if by some dainty god – was I not talking in my secret mind and thinking in my secret thoughts like a man? Well, fortunate then I was in my man's clothes.

As if well abreast of these thoughts she said:

'I see you got yourself a second pair of trews. I don't say I relished the last pair. You should've seen me returning to camp. Like a buck-naked child. Folks laughed till they wept.'

Then I was laughing again. 'Anyway I am told that gun be in your camp.'

'Well,' she said, 'you come down and we see about it.'

'You say?' I said. 'It may be that Wynkle King senior sold it to your bossman Mr Petrie. So I don't know if he'll want just to give it.'

'What were you planning to do to get it so?'

'I were planning to steal it.'

'Well, that always a good plan,' she said, and broke out laughing herself.

Chapter Seventeen

Nearer the encampment there was a picket every hundred yards. Colonel Purton's raid had put them on a war footing.

'Whiskey,' called out Peg each time we came close to one and of course that was her word of safe passage. I had dismounted anyhow and was leading the tired mule. He took a great suck of water out of the creek when he got down there. There was no moving him till he was satisfied. Peg was looking at him.

'That one thirsty critter,' she said, easy as you like, stroking his dark brown neck, a gesture the mule appreciated judging by the way he shivered his muscles.

'Best mule we ever had,' I said.

'You was riding him last time when I shot you, ain't that right? If I had known it was you I would not have shot you, Winona Cole.'

'Oh? Well, I was going to shoot you if I could have so I guess it makes no odds.'

We were just looking at each other. Simple. I was half glancing at the camp now and its five or six rough cabins. Plenty of horses tethered under the trees. Here come the summer flies, they were thinking maybe. Going to be shaking their fine heads and swishing their tails like the strange mechanisms of big fleshy clocks. Something about a horse or a mule touches the human heart. Goodly godly critters. There were no washerwomen this time but there was plenty to-ing and fro-ing in the camp. Even rebels got to make the stew. Looked at one way there was an air of paradise over everything. Birds have no allegiance to Union or otherwise so they were generous in their whistling and calling. The music of birds. I guess everything comes from that, the dances of simple country folk, the old songs that both cure and trouble the hearts of listeners. I want to say how I felt in that moment because I didn't think I had felt much like that before. I knew when gazing upon Thomas and John Cole there was a strong feeling of safety and regard. I would have spoken for them in any court before God or man. Before the Great Spirit herself. I would have said item by item all that they had attempted on my behalf, just as if I were their blood-attested daughter. I was a fragment, a torn leaf, torn away from the plains. Everything we were had been cleared off the earth. Without Thomas and John maybe there would have been only what the lawyer Briscoe called perdition – the sudden exit that followed a sentence of death. I might have starved out like one of those dried prairie dogs you find among the lupins and the grasses. Then that must have been a species of love. I never gazed upon Jas Jonski with much of feeling, except I was very curious to find what his kiss tasted like in my mouth, which I never did find, as far as I know. But gazing on Peg made my legs wash with flame. My stomach grew warm and I felt an infinite gratitude to the Great Spirit that Peg had been made, and set on the ground to live. It was as if to stand near her was to stand mid-current in the flow of a river.

I tied my mule under the trees by the stream because I couldn't walk him up to the unknown horses since there'd be mares or stallions maybe would unsettle him. A mule will not ever be a father or a mother, in my mule's case a father. Lige Magan used to tell a story about a chimera born to one of his grandfather's mules but that happened once in a hundred years, he said. Such an animal was considered to be the harbinger of fabulous harvests – 'Guess just not in our case,' said Lige philosophically.

Anyhow I walked up the rough river meadow to the houses side by side with Peg.

◑

I didn't think this could end well but what had brought me there, though still a mystery, I could *nearly* touch and itemise. A sense of it like you might sense a lion behind a rock. It hovered just beyond my reach of thought. The rifle certainly, but also other more ghostly things. It was reckless, reckless to be there in the first place. But being with Peg didn't make me uneasy. I never felt less uneasy since my mother's arms lay down my back and she unspooled her stories.

'I going to ask Aurelius what we can do about the gun. I know it was your gun because I seen it there on that mule. What's more you tried to shoot me with it.'

'Ain't Aurelius Littlefair – ?' I began, not sure how to proceed with that question.

'What?' she said.

'Ain't he a fierce sort of person?'

'Aurelius? He just what he is. Zach Petrie went off this morning early with his men so I can't ask him – unless you know how to spirit talk?'

'I don't.'

'Well, see, the armoury is up there beyond the last shed. If we got your gun it's there on a rack.'

'Like I say, Peg, money passed hands, I don't know . . .'

'You want to try or not? I don't care.'

'I afraid to talk to him, I heard – Peg, I heard he was hanging freedmen along the ways and I seen that and I don't know – maybe he just hang me.'

'Child, he ain't a demon. I tell you. He always good to

me. My father was his best scout during the war. They were close in like buddies. I just ask him. It can't hurt. I weren't thinking that Winona Cole were scared of anything or anyone.'

'I don't fear living things.'

'Well, he ain't dead, I can tell you, he ain't dead.'

So then we were up to the first little cabins of the living quarters. There were pantaloons and cotton front-button shirts and ladies' underthings and such like hung in festoons at the back of the cabins. I supposed those washerwomen had gone on regardless of raids or less important matters like that. Someone was cooking up a mess of oats in a huge black pot but there was no one tending that just then. For the horses I thought. Unless renegades crave oats too.

'You be waiting here, Winona, my friend. I go in and beard the demon.'

She treaded in across the porch on her bare feet and disappeared into the dark of the cabin. The windows were small, for defence. You could stick a rifle out through them would be about the size of it. The day even though it was only just summer had taken a turn to compete with the fire under the big pot for heat. I could feel the force of it touching my head and I wished I had thought of putting on a hat. Lige Magan's admonishing face swam inside my head. 'Now, Winona, what did I say, what did I say?' He was right to favour hats. A huge swamp of yellow light fixed down on the camp. The wide river seemed fattened with temperature. Brightly it pushed along, singing that pebble-song of rivers. My elation had persisted but now without Peg I began to fret a little, and wonder should I make my own path to the armoury and just grab that sacred gun. I wondered should I do that. Why would Aurelius Littlefair, the most evil and venal heart in Tennessee, want to give a gun back to Winona Cole? Had I said to Peg it belonged to Tennyson Bouguereau, a man that Aurelius Littlefair had seen fit to make an effort to destroy? Or, did I know now that it wasn't him at all, but Colonel Purton? And I thought, had Colonel Purton done that just to stir the nest, just to make an official document with the lawyer Briscoe that would warrant an attack? I supposed that could be the case. I was congratulating myself on this fancy when Peg poked her head out the door and told me to come in.

'Step lively there, soldier,' she said.

So I entered into the very hall of evil. So it seemed to me. There were many devils and creatures of dark ilk in my mother's stories – they were often the most cherished characters of us children. Cherished because they made us squirm and sway with fear. The room was bare, clean, and strangely to me like one of the lawyer Briscoe's well-kept rooms – before the Petrie gang burned them. There was an air of clemency and order. A line of regimented books sat on the shelf. The table was full of piles of paper all squared off and shipshape. There were maps and pictures – indeed, this Aurelius Littlefair, named for a philosopher emperor, was working on one of the maps with a red-leaded pencil. Making a line for something, I could not say. Like those men that ran the railroad right across Turtle Island with the stroke of a pencil. He didn't look immediately. Rather than a fiery creature with horns he was a sort of miniature general. He wore a light grey jacket and his beard was combed and his moustache carefully trimmed – I could somehow imagine him doing that, peering into a dim mirror, and clipping the hairs. Maybe singing the while. He was as trim as a boat. His grey hair went back across his sun-darkened face, and his eyes were grey. When he now looked up and smiled the only blemish was a mouth of forsaken teeth. Then he set his eyes on his work again and went on with the marking of the map.

'So what your name?' he said.

I could barely think fast enough and I nearly said Winona.

'Bill, sir.'

'You a bosom pal of my Peg?'

'Yes, sir.'

'How in the world you meet each other? Maybe that one of the mysteries of the world. How folks meet.

Nowhere to meet in all of Christendom but you say you meet.'

He drew some more, wetting the red lead with his blanched mouth, marking, circling. Then he seemed to be done with that task, and pushed himself and his chair back from the table, and tipped the chair onto its rear legs, and balanced there. Now I could see he wore high black boots so polished that the room wanted to nest in them, windowlight and shadows.

'My Peg she say that we got a rifle belonging to you. I find that strange, but if we do, I will be very content to return it to you. I don't ever like to think my men pick up things that don't belong to them unless by right of war. The spoils of war by long tradition are due to the trooper and the centurion, Mr Bill. Ten thousand years of human affairs don't gainsay that. I would be obliged to you to hear how you think we might have inadvertently come to be in possession of that gun?'

'I ain't quite certain of the facts around it, sir,' I said. 'I heard from a man called the Reverend Wynkle King that he had found my gun and sold it to Mr Petrie.'

'Sold it to Mr Petrie. Fancy. I'm acquainted with this reverend although I don't believe there's a bishop alive in America would allow that man his title in these times. Let us go to the armoury and have a look for this rifle.'

Peg now beamed with pleasure and seemed inclined

to think that all was going splendidly. I was expecting still at any moment for the talk to veer in the wrong direction. For there to be uproar and fisticuffs. But there had been nothing of the kind and now this elegant little man, who even Lana Jane Sugrue might have praised for his pristine *couture*, rose from his chair. His spurs rattled a muffled tune on the earthen floor, beaten flat and sprinkled with sawdust, maybe against spits.

The armoury was not locked nor even protected by a sentry and it was a little building just the same as the sleeping sheds except by some unknown means they had brought in very old gun cabinets gleaming with glass and wood. I had a feeling they had been *found* somewhere or were legitimised as proper spoils of war. Anyway the racks were filled with army muskets, repeaters like the Spencer, and other more ancient weapons. There were pots of gun-oil and well marshalled rags.

The little general looked along the rows.

'I think I know all our weaponry. Why, Mr Bill, many of these guns have stories – some even have legends attached. You see this one here?' he said, pointing at a long-barrelled rifle of some sort, with beautiful dragons chased into the breech. 'That one fought at Antietam under Lee, when Lee outdid McClellan even though that fool outnumbered us. McClellan's trouble was, Mr Bill, he could not count. I hope you have your numbers?'

'I do,' I said. I was nearly going to say I worked for the lawyer Briscoe but thankfully stopped myself.

'I regret that Peg is a child of the wilderness. Not because I chose that, but because history itself chose so. As soon as ever we may bring our cause to victory, I will be sending all the children to school. For education is the same thing as salvation. Without education we will have no citizens and no country. Do you see your gun?'

I walked along the cabinets. There were dozens and dozens of them. But a Spencer rifle is a particular thing of some beauty. Suddenly I saw it and my heart beat faster with joy, as if I had found a living thing from which I had been long separated. To search and search and then to find – it seemed to me that the experience of life had rarely that outcome. But there it was. Its old sleek self. I opened the cabinet door that squeaked against the intrusion and pulled down the rifle, and turned the breech-block over to check the name. There it was, *LUTHER*, cut in by a proper silversmith, all curlicues and flourishes.

'You got it?' said Peg, beaming.

'I do. I didn't believe I would,' I said, the weight of the rifle familiar in my hands.

'That an old Spencer carbine,' said Aurelius Littlefair. 'Seen better days.'

I was surprised to hear him say that. Maybe he was right. Maybe it wasn't as shining and new as I remembered it. Somehow Tennyson's pride in it had kept it new in my thoughts.

'Well, I am glad we were able to return your property, I am glad. I am regular glad,' said Mr Littlefair. 'It has your name engraved?'

'Not mine,' I said, showing it to him.

'Is that Luther then that nailed his ninety-five theses to the door at Wittenberg?' said Mr Littlefair.

'I thinking not that Luther. Luther Magan it's for.'

As soon as the word Magan was out of my mouth like a rat from a bolthole I regretted it. Aurelius Littlefair didn't immediately react. He looked back at Peg a moment and was nodding his head, and then he tapped a finger on the name. I was still holding the gun as if some unknown sergeant had cried out *Inspection, Arms*. Maybe I strengthened my grip on it then.

'Well, Magan. So Peg, you be friendly now with a boy knows Magans.'

'How so, Aurelius?' said Peg, not having a notion what he meant by it.

'Luther Magan, father of Elijah – yellowleg, just like those others with him. Traitors all. Let me see, ain't it John Cole? Ain't it something – something McNulty, an Irish poltroon? So now, you the young Indian lives with them? I think you are. But ain't you a girl? By the soul of Tach Petrie, God rest him, I think you are.'

'She ain't,' cried out Peg.

'Well, he is,' said Aurelius Littlefair, quite indignant.

This was not a conversation I could relish. I had no clear notion what to do but the blood came up into my face and I blushed like a person with heatstroke. Turning away, I naturally brought the rifle with me. Then I more or less burst forth from the armoury, leaping the few steps, and raced away down to the water. I knew it wasn't going to be much of a plan to try and gallop away from a settlement of renegades armed to the teeth, but I had no other inspiration. I was a girl with a gun and I was running and soon I would vault up onto the mule. That was my glorious plan. I heard someone rushing after me and felt they were about to overwhelm me. I was ready only for an assault. My whole back of me cringed to expect it. Oh Jesus. I would have said that Aurelius Littlefair was a demon of a runner, skinny snake that he was, and would fetch me and fillet me when he did. He would take the skin off my face and boil it in front of me, my eyes rolling in their hollows. I could feel his touch, I could feel his touch.

But it wasn't Aurelius Littlefair, it was Peg. I got to the poor mule. He reared back from my worrisome hurry.

'Let me go, let me go,' I said. 'You can't be catching me now. I ain't willing to be caught.'

'I ain't running after you, I running with you,' said

Peg. She stared into my face and nodded. 'I coming with you.'

If I had been given a choice of what was to happen then she coming with me would have been the rosette, the medal, and the prize. No doubt. Up the slope the camp that had seemed so quiet and empty was now teeming with faces and voices. Aurelius Littlefair was shouting that I was to be stopped. He was shouting at Peg to do that very thing. He knew that once I was among the trees only a forest fire could find me out. I jumped onto the mule's back and Peg scrambled up after me.

'Go, go,' I bid my mule, and kicked him on with fury, and he blundered out across the ford of the river, throwing up great fumes and blasts of water, and when he reached the far bank he took the slope like a champion. A mule is a person of great spirit, he will always try and serve you though it bursts his heart. Whether there were bullets after us I do not know nor hear them in memory – but I suppose even Aurelius Littlefair, killer of men and hanger of freedmen, would not fire on that rare and beauteous Peg.

Chapter Eighteen

On setting out I had tied the old holster to my mule in the dim hope it might carry the rifle home. Now it was, such happiness invaded me. The wandering folk that passed us on the road looked hungry and gaunt as ever. Even those on horseback didn't seem to understand what a high delight it was to be alive. My utmost dream had been to find the Spencer and there it was slugging in the holster.

At the back of my happiness was the thought that it might be a dangerous thing to be bringing Peg back to Lige's farm. If she thought so too she made no mention of it. She took my mood into herself and it seemed to us that even the birds of the woods were in accord with our happiness.

How long had I been so weighed down that I had forgotten this lightness of heart? After all, was I even eighteen years old? I didn't truly know. Born under the Full Buck Moon. Somehow with Peg behind me I felt I was returning not only to the place of refuge that was Lige Magan's farm but to a more distant place of safety.

Somewhere out on the plains of a country we didn't know was called Nebraska Territory or Wyoming but thought was called our heartland and a homeplace never to be lost. Where as a little child I had sat in safety with my mother and sister, enclosed in a teepee with all the magical symbols of protection marked inside and out. With all the grasses spreading away in every direction and sometimes the passing thunder of the buffalo and sometimes the silent thunder of the lupins with their clots of blue and purple flames. Returned not in body there of course. Better to say that feeling of simple freedom returned to me across the farmed and wild acres between me and Wyoming. Because I had been allowed by fate to find Tennyson's Spencer.

We were coming to evening now when all the colours were made simple in their hearts and all the browns were taken away and one sombre brown alone remained and all the blues. It was as if I had never seen this Tennessee with proper eyes. For Peg's people it had been their Wyoming. Maybe you could count the remnant Chickasaw on the fingers of a hand. But she in herself seemed to me to be a whole nation. Her beauty was a legion crowd.

How to say any of this to Thomas and John Cole? I did not know.

I knew that they might be out with the harrow pulling away weeds between the tobacco rows despite the day being Sunday. Beyond the eyes of preachers and priests. You couldn't get your hair cut on a Sabbath in Tennessee but weeds and hornworms didn't observe the holy days. The chapel of a hornworm is the tasty sand lugs. Maybe Lige Magan was topping and looping and so risking the two dollar fifty cent fine. Maybe Tennyson and Rosalee were patiently picking off the hornworms so as not to leave him alone in his disgrace. Maybe the wild animals passing unseen at the margins of the fields understood the urgent imperatives of crops and maybe the sun was so weak now it was engreying the vanishing woods and tempting out the field crickets. With their broken fiddles, as Thomas McNulty once said. I did not know. I did not know. It was a happiness to know nothing but the trotting of the mule and Peg's hands gripping my sides so tightly I thought she would surely tear my shirt. The warmth of her body now and then tipping against me so welcome I thought she might tear my heart. Tear it and mend it in the one breath.

◐

Sunday might be a good day for miracles or it might not. In our childish exultation were those little fertile seeds of worry. As we drew closer to the familiar woods and fields even the mule seemed to drag his hooves like a poor man who maybe had started out so sprightly on his gallows walk. Wanting to be brave since terror would not serve him well. Had I committed a daughterly crime by going back to the danger of the Petrie camp? How would I tell them who Peg was without further indicting myself in that regard? And why had I even been so fearsomely fixed on getting back the gun? A wagon of thought that drove itself on and on and myself only the hapless rider. What odds to Tennyson? as Lige Magan had said. And all the possible ruckus I might bring down now on all our heads. Well, I hadn't stolen Peg, she had stolen herself. She had stolen herself away. And it might be thought that I would be alarmed by that and not have a notion what to do with her next. But that didn't trouble me even for a moment. The stream reaches another stream and they mingle their waters as natural as you like, that was what it seemed. There was nothing in the girl astride the mule behind me that I feared.

We saw storm clouds moiling on the far mountains. But here in Lige's fields the sun had tried again to bleach bright greens to white. The effort of the day was felt in the relief thereof. Rest indeed. The scrubby land before the cabin, an acre of shallow soil too thin to plough, that was good only for an old mule out to pasture maybe, was the very ground over which Tach Petrie had tried to lead his men against us long ago. And he would have killed us all had we not killed him. That was sure. I heard the evening voices in the house. So their breaking of the Sabbath was done.

Tennyson Bouguereau was sitting on the porch in his accustomed corner. The redbud tree that someone had planted years ago was neither too dense nor scant. Its big flame of flowers burned without moving. I heard Rosalee talking suddenly loudly and laughing suddenly. It's a wonder all that talk that goes on in lives and never much considered or remembered. Never prompted too much by actual thought and no matter. Just the merciful birdsong of whatever bird we are.

I didn't know how much notice he was taking of me and Peg, arriving on the mule with stolid steps. Just the little thump of hooves on hardened ground. I clambered down in a strange excitement that seemed to include the necessity not to call out to him and hitched the mule and helped Peg down and reached for the heavy Spencer in its holster and dragged it out. Just then I glanced at Tennyson and I saw he had risen to his feet. I walked up to the porch holding the rifle across my right arm. Tennyson forsaking his bower came the length of the porch. He gave no hint of what he was thinking. He walked down the sere old steps. He came towards me quietly. We stopped near each other in the same moment. I nodded my head, and offered him the Spencer. Without hesitation he took it into his possession. He looked at it with the intelligence of the emperor Aurelius and touched the word *LUTHER* on the breech.

'I thank thee, Winona,' he said.

◐

The summer passed and Peg was decreed the finest picker of hornworms off tobacco leaves in the history of Tennessee – according to Thomas McNulty. It only took a day to know Thomas. John Cole was more difficult to know quickly.

Matters must have been moving and moiling according to their own ghostly rules. The new governor was turning everything about.

'As if yon war were never fought,' said Thomas McNulty.

We never had lived all easy in our minds at Lige's farm and we didn't expect any change in that.

We heard that Zach Petrie's camp over at West Sandy Creek was broken up and he went back with his followers to his great farm west of Paris. It was said it all lay in ruins and he would need a long course of work to mend it.

'Who he get to work that? No one. Ain't a sensible freedman touch him with a long stick.'

Late in the summer Aurelius Littlefair was appointed a judge of Henry County. The lawyer Briscoe shook his grizzled head.

'I got to plead a case before a hangman?' he said.

Things like that were said in his temporary quarters.

Now we wondered not only what would happen to us but what would happen to the likes of Colonel Purton. Rumour was the militia was to be disbanded.

Then in the town a freedman called Imre Grimm, who Rosalee knew because she had heard him speak at a meeting of the Freedmen's Bureau, was arrested. He was supposed to have attacked the pretty wife of a carpetbagger. Aurelius Littlefair didn't even get to put on his judge's suit. A bunch of citizens dragged Imre Grimm out of the jail. John Perry was told to bring his travelling forge. They stoked up the fire and hung Imre Grimm above the forge on a long chain. They cut off his fingers so he couldn't climb away. They cut off other parts. The whole town came out to see. Children too. When he was dead at length they divided up his blackened body for souvenirs.

'Now truly we are citizens of the devil's country,' said the lawyer Briscoe.

There was other news to hear shortly after. Sheriff Flynn threw in his work as sheriff and upped sticks and went down with his wife to Jacksonville in Florida. The mysterious troubles he was dealing with turned out to be his wife's illness. She had been consumptive for a long while and now the doc said she would die in another Tennessee winter. It was strange to me how he simply walked out of my story but I was also glad he loved her well enough for that. Yet it was one person less against the flood of Littlefair and his like. The lawyer Briscoe said that Sheriff Flynn had also been told that he would be killed if he didn't change his tune. The threats had come as a little run of nameless letters. The lawyer Briscoe said that in his opinion it could only have been someone in the pay of Littlefair.

'A *homo sacer* if ever there was one,' said the lawyer Briscoe. 'Any man could kill *him* now without penalty. And he a judge.'

When he said things like that I always felt a pang of disquiet for Peg. She had been a child of all that mayhem.

Next thing we heard, Frank Parkman himself was elected sheriff, though, as Lige Magan said, he wasn't much more than a boy. This was strange to John Cole, because Frank Parkman had ridden out so often with Sheriff Flynn, and might have been thought to be in cahoots with him. Not so, it seemed. But then no heart was clear, no soul was verified, in those times.

'Less we slaving black men and reining back the war the economy of Tennessee ain't nothing,' said the lawyer Briscoe, but he wasn't saying it to anyone especially.

In this strange time maybe it was Peg only keeping us from vicious harms. She didn't have her letters and I undertook to write a note for her to Zach Petrie, saying she was in good order and 'was in hopes to visit him soon'. Whatever was the reason, and we didn't trouble to think too deeply to find one, since there was no point, no expected posse of violent intent came to us. It was terribly strange to write a letter starting *Dear Mr Petrie*.

We slaved at our crops and the lawyer Briscoe now doubly defiant raised up his house.

He was intent on doing more than that too. He came out to talk to Lige one open-hearted summer's day. We sat with him on the porch where there was merciful shade. Peg had a caution against the lawyer Briscoe and chose to stay out of his way – she had set off into the woods with a gun when she saw him coming, thinking maybe to shoot something for supper. He said he had written to the Negro college in Nashville and it was a fact that freedmen of any age could attend there. He said they had a Negro band that travelled about the country raising funds and he thought that Tennyson having such a great fund of old songs might be very welcome there. Rosalee listened gape-eyed.

'My brother he can't do that, he got an injury,' she said quietly. Tennyson was out back somewhere but she maybe didn't know exactly where. His old chair at the end of the porch was empty anyhow.

'He can speak for himself on the matter, I expect,' said the lawyer Briscoe, in his brittlest voice.

'I speak for him since he can barely speak for hisself,' said Rosalee, rolling back the ball.

But Tennyson was strengthening day by day. We had all heard him singing again at his work. He had so many songs, not just the sweet old work songs, but other things, and I loved when he sang 'The Famous Flower of Serving Men'. He was talking just about the same as before, despite what his sister said. Now for Lige this was in the country of miracles but of course also he needed Tennyson desperately to work the farm with him and the others. It was long hours of struggle as it was. Good struggle, but struggle.

'I can't say I am so filled with joy to hear you say this,' said Lige doubtfully.

'We got to take him out of danger,' said the lawyer Briscoe. 'He ain't safe here in Henry County. No, sir, he ain't.'

The lawyer Briscoe's face was even redder than it used to be. It was like the great conflagration had reddened him on a permanent basis. He had said the last words with that rush of righteous anger I knew so well in him. When his ideas were gainsaid. But he also could ride past that anger and leave it behind for what it was, a toothless snake in the grass.

'I ain't fixing to leave you worse off than before but that man needs taking out of here, that what I can say.'

'No one of us be safe now,' said Lige, in the quiet voice of truth.

'If I can say,' I said, thinking this was the time to say it, 'I heard it was Colonel Purton struck Tennyson, not the Petries.'

'Where you hear that, Winona?' said Thomas McNulty.

Even John Cole laughed as if I had said the craziest thing on the menu.

'I sorry, Winona,' he said, 'you snuck up on me with that one.'

'Maybe she heard right?' said Thomas McNulty, affronted at John Cole.

'That can't ever be,' said the lawyer Briscoe.

Just then Peg came round the cabin with a brace of rabbits on her back. She looked pretty wild with her long black hair and her gun and the rabbits dangling there forlorn of life. The lawyer Briscoe nodded at her. He didn't say anything about her. But he was looking at her with that head-turned-sideways look of his.

'I best be going. God help an old man in this heat,' he said.

Then he was walking down to his buggy and stirring up the horses stunned by sunlight.

Rosalee was silently crying in her seat.

Chapter Nineteen

As if the threat to Lige of losing Tennyson wasn't enough, now John Cole went down with the illness that assailed him now and then. He went down to the letter of the phrase – collapsed suddenly midstride as he came back in from the fields. Then it was Thomas McNulty and Tennyson carrying him into his room like a wounded warrior. His face was the white of a lily and all his long thin self as bendy as a pair of trews. They heaved him into the bed. They knew all they could do was wait and attend him.

We were already cutting sand lugs and so it was myself and Peg with the big knives chopping the finished leaves and Lige and Thomas dragged them to the wagon. A sand lug is as heavy sometimes as a stone, there's a deal of hauling and cursing to harvest them. Maybe Peg looked like only half a girl in body weight but she was strong, I would aver. She might have wrestled a mountain lion and made it wish it had kept to its mountain.

When you hold a person in high regard it is a great pleasure just to gaze on them, just to look at them moving through the normal air of a day, just to notice how they have a habit of this or that, the turn of a hand or how maybe the person, this person that you revere, turns up their chin, or raises their arms to put a tie on their hair. Even their anger can be a kind of strange elixir. Their strength is like something good said among people.

◐

Just as I had done for Peg, it was a preacher called Jodocus Troutfetter who wrote a letter for Jas Jonski, even though as far as I knew, he had gone to school in Nashville. He was always writing at Mr Hicks's store, long lines of orders for this and that. Maybe that wasn't the same thing as speaking your heart. Speaking your heart is the devil of a business. Straight talking might do the job for Peg but the reverend wasn't so minded. I kept this letter because there was something in it that put me in mortal fear – I didn't understand it, maybe, and then, I did:

My dear Winona Cole,

This missive is being written down by the Rev. J. Troutfetter at the express direction of Mr Jas Jonski Esq. of Paris, TN, originally of the city of Nashville. Though indeed I have my letters, I fear I might not by my own means express the truth. Dear Winona, pursuant to the love I feel for thee and in reference to our recent desire for a worthy betrothal in the Methodist church of Paris, TN, I hereby and to thee declare that my wish and love remain <u>*intacter*</u> *and that if there have been events to draw regret from a human heart I profess to possession of same and wish in all amplitude & greatness of spirit to REPEAT and REINSTATE my vow to love thee and marry thee before the gathered congregation of the elders, ministers, preachers, and members of the above said church.*

'For a man may sin and yet be brought to good.'

Again and again I say to thee I have only REGRET for any harm you believe done to thee, for which harm I hereby allocate a sense of PENANCE & SORROW and hope you will see fit again to GATHER ME TO THY BOSOM and altogether UNITE with the fond and remorseful undersigned, JAMES HENRYK JONSKI.

Then he signed it, and scribbled in what looked like his own hand: *Please Winona I do love you.* Maybe he thought that was the clincher. Maybe he meant everything he said.

He had sent it to me at my place of work, viz. the lawyer Briscoe's. I read it at my little table newly set up in the barn. When I looked up from the pages the lawyer Briscoe's head was cocked sideways, looking at me. He didn't say anything, he didn't ask about the letter, though he might have, if he assumed it was on his business. If you can hide the fact that a bladed wind is blowing through you, I did. I felt as small as a wren. I felt the world was just a great boulder pressing on my body. It might be as well to give way to it, to let it crush me, I thought. The religious lingo was a blade to slay me. For a moment I felt I would have to marry him not because there was an ounce of me that wanted to, but because of the official terms I had been addressed with, like a treaty paper between Washington and the Sioux.

On the way home I gave it to Lige and asked what he thought of it and he read it right there with the reins loose on the mare's back and the animal shuddering with a desire to head home.

'The Reverend Troutfetter – don't believe I know that fella,' he said, and folded the letter and put it back in its cover. 'You read that to John Cole. He'll know what to do.'

The land was trying to loosen itself from the royal heat of summer. The mare plodded along. When we were within a hundred yards of the cabin I leapt down from the traverse and ran along the track to the house.

●

John Cole was very sombre as I asked could I read the letter to him. Of course he was so weak he couldn't even raise his head. Thomas McNulty added to the hump of his pillow an old army jacket and then John Cole was ready to assist me.

I was afraid to have Thomas listening in the room because he was still able-bodied and I still had a terror of him going off to town in rage. The rage of Thomas McNulty was very simple. It happened seldom but when it did it was like the anger of the righteous angels. He knew the absolute menace of the world. He knew it was a place so knotted with evil that good could only hope to unknot a tiny few threads of it. But he was a man that believed in the great freeing possibility of the untoward good outcome of matters. He would give his life for that. In fact he thought he was obliged to and many times nearly had. My safety was the second article of his religion. The state of John Cole, to which he brought soups, and the first berries of fall, and warm water so he could bathe him in the bed, was the first. After all without John Cole he wouldn't have been inclined to see a purpose in life. They had walked in destitution through ruin and destruction many times. They had found this verdant haven with Lige Magan, their old comrade in arms. It was all the one. Where John Cole abided, there was to be found Thomas with his simple heart. Their love was the first commandment of *my* world – Thou shalt hope to love like them. We have all to meet many souls and hearts along the way – we are obliged to – we must pray we can encounter one or two Thomases and John Coles on that journey. Then we can say life was worth the living and love was worth the gamble.

Thomas was quite content to let me alone with John Cole, indeed he was. Indeed, he said, he thought I *should* be alone with him.

'I just go and feed those damn mules,' he said. 'I'll feed them good oats for the work on the morrow.'

Then he was just on the cusp of going and then it seemed to me he was hoping I would change my mind and tell him not to go and then when I did not, he went.

So I read the letter to John. He nodded and nodded the while. He was listening hard. When I finished I looked at his quiet face and thought again that for a rough boy who had walked out of New England as a child and was the great-grandson of an Indian and as poor as ever man was he sure was a fine-looking person. He could have run a country if anyone had so asked him. His head was missing the inch in its width that maybe a normal head would have – it was narrow, like a little gap between dwellings. He was a shadow person – a place of shadows.

All as gentle as a child with me and all as fierce as a buffalo in battle. John Cole, the keel of my boat. Thomas the oars and the sails.

'I do know how that strike me,' he said, his words as sombre as his face. I could hear the strange moisture of his illness trying to stop the words in his throat. He said nothing for a long while. He was struggling to surface from a deep deep pool of difficulty. Then his face opened again like that spot in the woods touched suddenly by stray sunlight.

'It strike me as a confession,' he said at last.

●

Weeks went by and then Colonel Purton in all his military glory arrived at the farm. I could swear he had added more braid and silver to his uniform as if to suggest the grave anxiety he felt, an anxiety clearly expressed in his strange dark face. He was like a man just awoken from sleep. His very words seemed heavier to him, and slower. I was beginning to wonder had something assailed him, an apoplexy or the like. Sure enough his left arm seemed useless to him, and he rode with the reins gripped oddly in the right. He had never been out to Lige's before but of course Lige knew him well enough. Lige liked to know the people he was expected to talk to. The colonel had ridden down to the house in the company of twenty militia men, single file like a black snake. With all the turning about of recent events Lige Magan was inclined quietly to prop a rifle on the porch, as if it always rested there. It was just near noon and the sun was at his most endowed. Such a blaze of light covered the ragged acre even though we were stepping deeper into the year. The men had been in for a feed and had larrupped down without discrimination anything even only cousin to food that Rosalee put in front of them. We were in the midst of the main harvest and there was plenty to do, a fact that sat in our faces too, giving us that stunned idiot look of harvesters.

Tennyson the previous night had gone off in the darkness towards Paris. Lige Magan had given him one of the mules despite a mule being a more needed creature than a man. But Tennyson had undertaken to send the mule back with a boy for twenty cents. Oh yes, a good mule was gold. Anyhow we had walked out to track with him into the wagon road. He had had his possessions in saddle bags across the rump of the mule and his Spencer was concealed under a cloth. We didn't know what a college would make of a new student arriving thus but needs must in that ferocious time.

I don't need to itemise the grief of Rosalee in losing her brother though as Lige Magan said, 'they didn't build

Nashville too far from Paris.' This was small sop to Rosalee. Being a person of infinite feeling she tried her best to contain those feelings in her breast, she tried almost to bursting. She had accepted the wisdom of Tennyson trying his hand at 'Fisk' – the name of the college. There was no doubt he was a beautiful singer. And as people who had earned their livelihood from the hall in Grand Rapids, that is to say, Thomas McNulty, myself and John Cole, in the long ago, we felt a strange envy of Tennyson's adventure. But *here* was a place where the whirring blades of our story might cut him to pieces. *There*, in unknown Nashville, he might flourish and blossom. He was certainly a rose among men. We had walked back in silence all the same to the cabin.

So now we were a good man short, the best worker Lige had, and Lige was wanting to get back out into the tobacco crop.

Nevertheless Lige didn't feel he could leave the colonel and his men sweltering in that furnace noon, so everyone trooped into the parlour till it was just bodies wall to wall. Rosalee asked Colonel Purton would he take anything to drink or eat and the colonel begged of her water for him and his men.

As she went out on this errand I heard her mutter to herself: 'What a terrible stink of men.'

'We like kittens burning on a bonfire,' he said.

He looked like no kitten that ever a cat had spawned.

'We was sad to hear about Sheriff Flynn going to Jacksonville,' said Lige.

'For all I can see I the only true authority left in this forsaken county,' he said, 'unless you like to take your orders from renegades and rebels.'

'So Frank Parkman, he don't get your vote?' said Lige Magan.

'Frank Parkman? Not when he signs up young Wynkle King as his deputy, not when he does that, no, sir.'

'Well that don't sound like much of a protection against the evils of the world,' said John Cole, recently 'risen from the dead' as Rosalee put it, but still weak.

'What going to be the outcome of all this?' said Lige. 'You got a notion of that?'

'Outcome is, I can get no notice of intent from the governor nor anyone other. Outcome is, Aurelius Littlefair a goddamned judge of the US circuit court. Outcome is, every freedman best watch his back, or,' he said, accepting a mug of spring water from Rosalee, 'her back. That the outcome.'

'Ain't Tennessee this long time in the Union and all that settled?' said Thomas McNulty, in his most serious voice.

The colonel leaned back in his chair in so much as he could in such a crowded company.

'No,' he said.

Some of the militia men laughed, not because it was intended to be humorous, but just maybe at the bluntness of the colonel.

'Anyhow,' the colonel said, 'I come out with other things of import. That young boy Jas Jonski been killed.'

Chapter Twenty

I was trembling then. As if all the story of Jas Jonski was an electric eel and it had stung me.

Did I feel a moment of sorrow for him? I did. Maybe a few moments. But then I asked myself, why was Colonel Purton going to the trouble of coming out to tell us this? Dread flooded into every crevice of my body. In an instant Peg stepped an inch closer to me. I could feel her tense body in a long seam against mine. It was as if someone had tipped a cup of poison into my mouth. I pushed out through the men because I felt my belly boiling. Out on the sere grass I vomited up my vittles. I bent over like a bow and vomited. I was panting like a hurried mule.

'You white as a whiteman,' said Peg, standing gingerly by me, her hand on my hot back.

'I can't – talk,' I blurted, and vomited again.

There's nothing elegant about vomiting, that's a fact.

Colonel Purton came out after us as if maybe he was thinking he had best keep the rabbit near since he *had* the rabbit near. But the truth was I had no idea what was in his head. Shades and shadows were his business. Quiet creeping along shadow-frequented ways. He said to Peg he would be much obliged if he could have a few words with me alone. Peg asked me with a look if that was all right, I wordlessly said it was. So I sat down on a withered old stump and tried to wipe the vomit off my face as best I could. My hair was still kept short so at least that wasn't dreeping with the stuff.

The colonel surprised me by kneeling down beside me – as if he meant to propose marriage. That was not what was on his mind of course. It brought his head just about level with mine. I thought he meant to seem harmless by so doing. I can't say he succeeded in that.

'You like to wear them trews,' said the colonel, 'I remember. But I know you a girl. You Winona Cole, John Cole's daughter. I talking to the lawyer Briscoe and he telling me about you. And oh, he don't care to say too much, because he has the discreet manners of a lawyer.'

He shifted on his knee. I guess the ground was a little hard and hot for him, and his knees weren't young.

'Jas Jonski he killed about midnight last night. Someone just stuck a knife into him. Stuck a knife in maybe twenty times. He all covered in blood of course. No matter, he maybe died at the first strike, Dr Tharpe says, he don't know, but he supposes. Long thin blade into the heart anyhow, one of them. Very, you understand, missy, precise – expert you might say.'

He was looking at me all the while to see how I was reacting. I wasn't exactly smiling but I wasn't not smiling either. I thought, you have got to keep an even keel, Winona. You have got to remember how dangerous the world is and that here is a mighty patch of danger and you have got to live through it. Be wise, Winona, and live through it. Trouble always comes and no use wishing it didn't. Thing is, to get through it – and out the other side. If there is another side.

'I guess I was told by someone that you like to carry a knife? Many Indians do maybe. You carry one?'

I bent to my right boot and pulled out my knife and held it out to him.

'That a long thin blade, right enough,' he said. 'Can I look closer at it? You don't mind?'

I nodded and he took the sharp thing and then he held it closer to his eyes and squinted and I guess he thought he saw something there.

'You see this, missy – just a mess of red along the blade? You see that. It hard to see.'

'That blood,' I said.

'That blood, that right, whose blood though?' he said. 'Whose?' he said again, sounding like one of our familiar owls.

'That me skinning rabbits for Rosalee. She bring them in and then I skin them. Peg don't like to skin, she don't got the knack of it.'

'But you do? You an expert with the knife?'

'Not so bad.'

'You not thinking that this the blood of that boy Jas Jonski?'

He said it like a bit of idle talk, real easy.

'No. I ain't thinking that because it ain't. I don't care for Jas Jonski maybe but I ain't inclined to kill him either. I never killed no one.'

'You killed the famous Fat Man worked for Tach Petrie. I heard you did. You killed him, with your little señorita gun.'

'That were in a battle. In a fight.'

'You think love ain't a fight? In my experience, love, love the biggest fight there is, right enough.'

Then he seemed to turn away from this thought.

'I want to believe you, missy, but in my line of business belief's not worth much. The lawyer Briscoe say you a clever person though, I grant you, his best boy, he called you – even though you a girl.'

Then Colonel Purton laughed a strange metallic laugh.

'Lawyer Briscoe know me as well as anyone.'

'Oh, yes, he vouches for you, he does. And I say to you I like that man. He as straight as a mason's plumb line, he is. No doubt. So, missy, let's say you the innocent party, then let's ask ourselves, all right, if it weren't no bright clever Indian girl in a pair of boy's trews, then who? Here's a few names. Now you the friend of all these people here,' and he gestures towards the cabin behind him, 'so I don't expect you to speak against nobody. I will say the names and I will look in your pretty brown eyes and you will tell me what you thinking just by some small movement. You ready?'

'I don't know who might have done it.'

'That's fine, that's fine. Now – Tennyson Bouguereau. How about him? He were seen in town last night.'

'That's because he was staying with his friend before he catch the train to Nashville in the morning early.'

'He took a train to Nashville?'

'He did. He going to a big college there. The lawyer Briscoe got that for him. Likely he don't go killing a man afore he catches a train.'

'The lawyer Briscoe, huh?'

'Yeh, a boy just brought back the mule this morning. Gave him twenty cent for the work.'

'See, I thinking if I can just find out who killed Jas Jonski maybe I find out who killed other folk, or who might kill other folk in the coming future. That how my mind working. Hope you don't object to me being so open with you. The general state of peace and death is militia business. Now Sheriff Parkman if I may so call him he the one said you were skilled with a knife.'

'I don't see how he would know that,' I said.

'He said you threatened to stick a knife in him one time – maybe this knife,' he said, handing it back to me. I stuck it straight in my boot. 'That ain't true?'

'That ain't even a small bit true,' I said, 'I said—' But it seemed to me too complicated to say what I said and why I said it that time in the livery, since it involved the offering of a kiss.

'Anyhow – all right – let's try some other names. I going to look in your eyes now when I say them. Lige Magan. Lige Magan hisself. How you feel about Lige?'

He was watching my eyes like a hovering hawk.

'Not much,' I said.

'See I know if you think I come close to something your eyes going to *hop*. Like a rabbit, like one of those rabbits you talking about. Skinning, you said. With your little knife. Well, outside the town you gotta skin rabbits, I know that. So that's how I'll skin this rabbit. All right – so let me say the name of that old boy in there, now I don't know him, but he was a felon, that I know, and I heard other things about him that I don't know what to say about. Thomas McNulty.'

He was staring, staring. I was locking my eyes let me tell you.

'Now, how you feeling about – well, I should say first Rosalee Bouguereau, but if I get a hop for her I don't know but I'll – I think I'll cancel Christmas. Anyhow how you feeling about John Cole. John Cole? I don't get no hop for that? I think I should. Maybe Injun eyes just don't behave like whiteman eyes. I don't know.'

He rose creakily from his knee and rubbed it under the black cloth.

'Anyhow, good to talk to you. I can see how clever you are. I suppose commiserations are in order on the death of your fiancé.'

'He weren't. He was, but then he weren't.'

'Well. I have to tell you, missy, that Sheriff Parkman favours you for the crime. But I don't know if I do.'

Then he went over to Peg where she was hiding as she thought out of sight in the bushes at the side of the house. And he spoke to her and I couldn't hear what they were saying. But I could tell it wasn't just as friendly as my talking to him. He stood over her in an ugly way and waved his fist at her. So then he walked back to the cabin and called out his men and off they went in a sudden pall of grey dust.

I asked Peg what he had said to her.

'He said he knew who I was and had a notion to whup me but it was just too damn hot, that's what he said.'

'Maybe he thinking you killed Jas Jonski.'

'Maybe I did. Then he asking did Winona Cole, that you, go to town last night and I told him that you went sleeping not too long after dark,' said Peg, 'which was nearly true.'

'It was true,' I said. 'You was beside me in the bed.'

'Well, yes indeed, but, we weren't all the time sleeping.'

'No, that true.'

●

'Yes, yes, he ask us all the same questions, where was you at such and such a time, and that thunderous crowd of silent militia men watching, watching, goddamn it,' said Thomas McNulty, looking as glum and frightened as a chicken when the hungry yardwoman sneaks close to try and throttle it.

John Cole though not yet a recovered man was all the same pacing up and down the parlour like he was trying to race his shadow.

I knew just why they were so dismayed. For ten years they cared for me and watched over me. Even when Starling Carlton stole me away on his own business, Thomas followed, crossing all the way from Tennessee to Wyoming. We were doing about forty miles a day, he was maybe a little slower and anyway got a late start. He didn't find me till Wyoming. I wondered how he had suffered, going all that way, not even knowing if he would ever find me again. His heart thumping ten times a day at the thought of failure. And John Cole waiting back at Lige's like maybe he was going to be thinking Thomas let him down – Thomas just thinking that, and the snake-venom of that thought poisoning his blood. It's a long way to go and never to question your love. That was the measure of Thomas McNulty. But you can't watch over your children for evermore. Day dawns when a child has to watch over himself. I knew well I had reached that time some time back. I surely had. Now all I could see was the torture in Thomas's face and the forced march of John Cole's pacing. It was a terrible sight to me. But they knew I was in trouble deep. They knew. Colonel Purton had told them too, Sheriff Parkman was of the confident opinion it was me that killed Jas. That's what he said, over and over, to each of them as he questioned them. 'I don't maybe think so, but that what he thinking,' he said, the colonel, over and over. He that likely struck down Tennyson just to make a signed paper to go get Zach Petrie. More than likely. Pity Tennyson never clapped eyes on him, and could say. Guess Colonel Purton was lucky that way or that was just how things fell.

Here was the big moment, the moment when I would sort things out for myself. But now here was Peg, my handsome, lithesome, perfect Peg, all run into the equation. I beheld the fright and fear of those I loved and revered and my own heart quailed in my chest. I looked over at my Peg all sweet and hard in the same breath and I wondered at the folly of God that He wanted these things to happen to me when it would have been easier to ignore me, go round me to the next girl, even to forgo me and assign me in the upshot to some whiteman's hell. I was almost happy to go there if by going Thomas and John would be assuaged and Peg would not be heartbroken. But there are some things that have only a splayed hand of outcomes and none of them good. That's what it felt like. The deep fear of the buffalo when it's being ridden down, the hunter close as a thought, and the barrel of a gun on the very cusp of issuing deathly fire. That balancing strange moment before death. The eyes bulging out with terror and anger. That's what it felt like, in that moment. Maybe the buffalo has her finest moment then, a moment of bright clarity, when all she loves is made plain to her, the prairie, the lupins, the harsh grasses, the long gasp of winter and the sudden bounty of spring. Made plain just in the second before she loses it.

'You the folks I attend to best in this world,' I said at length, 'but now I ask you to sit you down at that table and I will try and tell you what I am going to do.'

Chapter Twenty-One

The curious part of that night was the great storm that blew up out of nowhere and walked across our farm. Big lakes of water hung up in the very air were let loose on the dry earth. Long turning rollers of wind drove against the woods and the woods howled in their agony of protest. That was a terror in itself that it would flatten the corn and there was a sense of blessing in the fact that the tobacco was by then nearly all saved, leaf by heavy leaf. It was most of it bound on the big sticks in the barn. That barn was caulked better than the cabin, and now that Colonel Purton was gone off and the land had decided to give itself a mighty drenching, grounding the very dust his horses had raised, the rain found out every little gape and torn spot in the roof where the shingles had curled in the summer sun. It was the drip-drip-drips then, all over the parlour, over Thomas and John Cole's heads, over Lige's dusty boots, over Rosalee's game pie that she had heaved onto the table. She was making a brave attempt to keep everything as ever and always. A woman so ravaged by presages and presentments found it trebly grievous to live through such moments of clear disaster. I thought, she has had enough of them lately – truly she has. No one said anything about the deluge, not a word.

•

When years before Thomas gave himself over to the law and was brought up to Leavenworth to be tried for desertion he did it because he didn't wish to have more guns, outlaws, or lawmen near where I abided. At the time I was still a child. The first law for Thomas and John Cole had been theretofore flight. All their born days they fled from dangers and when they found new ones they did their best to break free and flee again. But then I was in their care and Lige's farm was considered a refuge before all in a time when everywhere was danger so it made no odds where you fled to and it was better to stand your ground with some close hearts and a few rifles. Anyhow running is a young man's game. Though not old in years exactly I knew the weariness in John Cole required a mode of nursing from Rosalee and Thomas – even Lige had mopped that brow betimes – and there was something in Thomas that spoke of age even if it wasn't written so much in his face. Men with hard beginnings pay cents on the debt that at length burgeon up to dollars. Though accounted a beauty in his youth it was a mortgaged beauty now. The rats of age were gazing on him from the shadows. Therefore it wasn't a time for running that would bring likely more ruin against their door.

I instructed them with my sternest voice they were to do nothing on my account. They were to let me do for myself. When Thomas held up a hand to protest, I held up my fiercest sword of words. Peg laughed at my ferocity but I told her also to remain where she was. Nothing besides my own case was more precarious than hers. She being in effect a child of a renegade people.

●

If you could make honey hover in the air it would be Peg. If you could take a sliver of the wildest river and make it a person it would be Peg. If you could touch your lips against a pulsing star it would be Peg. The long, soft, sweet, fierce, dancing, piercing, kissed form of her. With all the sweetness at the centre and all her limbs radiating out like the light of that very star and her face like the best likeness of a goddess but also the face of the most desired person in all the history of the world. So that when I desired her and beheld her I melted against her and was no more and not even truly Winona any more for all the long hours of the night.

●

I knew it was time to talk to the lawyer Briscoe in a way I had not managed before. In every story, he would say, there is a good man. The grace of the lawyer Briscoe was that he was the good man in his own story.

As I rode to see him in the aftermath of that storm – half of Tennessee strewn across the muddied road, great wheel-gouges hewn into the soil as carts and wagons struggled to make way as usual – I greatly desired to run, in spite of my own thoughts. It was morning now but the day itself seemed sluggish and reluctant to appear. I began to wonder what it would be like to make that old journey again to Wyoming and try and find Lakota like me who would welcome me back – maybe Peg too. I thought of the journey I made with Starling Carlton and how he pushed the horses till they were well nigh dead and indeed when finally we reached Fort Laramie his own horse so shattered and ruined he shot it. There were trains now if you were rich that would go even from Paris over to St Louis and then across all that strange majesty and length of miles to the high plains. It would be me and Peg on Lige's worst horses, we couldn't be expecting Pegasus and Bucephalus. Three weeks of travelling and creatures to be shot along the way to eat and now the year dipping deeper into itself and soon maybe snow higher up and the start of that sharp killing wind across the plains. And glowering darkness of skies and unfriendly moons staring down. And maybe Lakota people not so glad to see a Chickasaw and one that spoke nothing but English and knew nothing of the work of a camp. They might like her skill with a gun, they might. But was there anyone there who would know me? I could not think so. Many years and many battles and everything torn from its old place and all the hunger and outrage and terror of that life.

The last wind of the storm tossed across the way and a sunlight prickled through the thinning dark.

Maybe the lawyer Briscoe was half expecting me. Maybe from an instinct formed from what he knew of me and his own lawyerlike self. He sat me down. He asked Lana Jane Sugrue to bring us coffee. We could hear outside the doors of the barn the sounds of Joe and Virg banging with axes trying to clear up from the storm. The new roof was on the new house. An old tree had fallen but out of respect for the work had missed the house. Banging, banging, in a firm brotherly rhythm. Lana Jane Sugrue came back smiling with the cups, and set them down.

'Now, dear,' she said to me, and then went away again. Going out through the huge barn door she looked like a mouse going through the wainscotting.

I said I was so glad the house was nearly finished. He thanked me for the work I had done for him. He said he had been fortunate to have such a fine clerk of works. I thanked him in turn. This little conversation had the strain in it of being a thread to something else.

'Colonel Purton said he was talking to you,' I said.

'He came by,' said the lawyer Briscoe.

'Then you will know Jas Jonski is dead.'

'He said so.'

'And that Sheriff Parkman thinking I done it.'

Now the lawyer Briscoe made no answer to that.

'Mr Briscoe, would it be horrible to you if I sit here as your old acquaintance . . .'

'Old acquaintance, Winona – why, you my friend.'

'Your friend?'

'I hope so.'

This surprised me greatly, the sudden use of this word.

'I have been made greatly unhappy by circumstances,' I began, sounding in my own ears like someone far far away, in a novel, in England, say. 'I not saying anything to anyone except Rosalee Bouguereau, till now. But I have a fear that Frank Parkman will come arrest me.'

'I think he might,' said the lawyer Briscoe. He abandoned his coffee cup and got up and went to his famous cabinet, happily a survivor of the fire, and pulled down his very best whiskey and poured himself a glass. 'You know,' he said, 'my own nerves have not been the best lately. Greatly disturbed by circumstances, as you say.' He took a sharp draught of the gleaming yellow liquid. 'So,' he said. 'Your story.'

'You know that Jas Jonski was once my – I was once to marry him.'

'I might have known that,' he said, 'certainly.'

'And then I didn't wish to marry him and then he wrote just recent asking me again and John Cole said there was something in the letter more than Jas intended.'

'What was that?'

'A confession.'

'To what?'

I sat there willing my mother into my body, willing her to take me over and give me her famous courage. But all I managed to do was cry. It was not proper crying, it was as if moisture was being forced out through my eyes. The lawyer Briscoe as a substitute for leaning forward to comfort me, leaned back. It worked just as well. Slowly my stupid eyes stopped pumping tears. Slowly I calmed. And then some other thing took hold of me, some kind of fierce command. I felt suddenly as free as a freedman – that I could say anything in this new freedom. My mother, I thought, my mother.

'In the days when he was still my beau he hurt me,' I said slowly, trying to find the proper words. 'He hit me and marked my face.'

'I did know that, if you remember,' said the lawyer Briscoe. 'That was most dreadful. That carries a penalty of two years' hard labour if effectively proven. I did advise – restraint. Perhaps I was wrong. I may think now I was.'

'At the centre of this was something much worse, or that seem so much worse to me, and that has caused me—'

'Great unhappiness,' he said.

'Yes.'

'Winona, if we are referring to what I think we are, Blackstone tells us that the Saxons punished this crime with death. These later ages have been more lenient. The whole section in Blackstone makes for very curious reading. Some will say that *raptus mulierum* cannot occur within marriage, and it is commonly believed that a person affianced cannot experience it, but that such a circumstance comes possibly within the realm of fraud, which is deemed a misdemeanour, punishable also by hard labour. But I have never seen it so carried through. On the other side, you are as a Sioux person technically a prisoner of war of the new reservations in Wyoming and Montana, and as an Indian at large you may be deemed beyond civil law, or without law. Therefore it will be wholly a matter of outlook, opinion, and the general common law of a district, how much weight will be given this crime against you. Many will say it cannot be a violation.'

Then he took another draw of his whiskey. He had strangely warmed to this offered thinking as I had heard him so often before, with a client.

'However,' he said, 'this is all for nothing, because the truth is, I believe it was a violation. I believe it was a most severe and terrible violation, Winona, and knowing you, an astounding assault on your most excellent and unusual nature. And if I had known I might have with a clear conscience killed him myself.'

With this passionate speech ejected he stopped and began to weep himself. I had never seen the lawyer Briscoe weeping, even when his house burned down. I sat there in front of him watching the tears flow down his reddened face. Then he made a supreme effort, like a person might try to close a barn door in a high wind blowing against it, and smoothed a hand over his white hair.

'Well,' he said.

I could barely speak, but there was more to say, so I tried to say it.

'Frank Parkman on another occasion was told I had a knife – it was I myself that told him – and as it was a knife was the weapon used on Jas Jonski, and Frank Parkman his good friend, I think this is why he believes me to be the culprit.'

I expected him to ask, and are you? But he did not.

'Although he has not said it to me in person yet, but only Colonel Purton he has said it – and Colonel Purton, I know he is your friend, Mr Briscoe, and a man you give your best whiskey to when he comes, but he is a man I not trusting as good as I might.'

'No man is *entirely* trustworthy,' said the lawyer Briscoe, in his best sage voice. 'No man, alas.' And his face drifted away a moment to other days, it seemed to me. Then he banished the thought and was back.

'If Sheriff Parkman fashions an indictment,' he said, 'and arrests you and brings you to jail and you are arraigned for trial and are tried, why, I will defend you with every atom of my being. Every atom.'

He rose again and put more of his most precious whiskey into his glass, and talking to the cabinet rather than to me, said: 'I most certainly will. I most certainly will.'

◐

Now the fallen tree was cleared and the workmen had come in a long time since and the new house was a huge instrument of banging and tapping and men calling to each other. Just because the work was there to do I put the week's wages in order and pegged the urgent orders to the wall and the three boys we had for clearing up after jobs I sent in all directions to hunt up items that were late or gone astray. Work like that drives nearly every other thought away and there was the usual strange solace of numbers in spite of all.

I begged of the lawyer Briscoe that I might not go home that night. He undertook to find out what he could in Paris and off he went. By nightfall he was still away. Lana Jane Sugrue was one of those old-fangled people who rose with the dawn and went to bed near twilight, for want of a candle or a lamp. She did not lack for candles or lamps now but the habit had stayed with her. She was happy to show me a corner of her own bed. In truth she didn't take up much room in it anyhow but was only the length of a few feet under the coverlets, like a child. I was as hollow as a reed after my long talk with the lawyer Briscoe. I was very content to get in beside her and give way to sleep.

The next morning the lawyer Briscoe said that Sheriff Parkman appeared to have gone off to Nashville on business – he knew not what business. Jas Jonski's mother had already buried her son. The lawyer Briscoe had spoken to Deputy Wynkle King and the deputy said that I had been seen in town that night – 'that little Injun girl,' he called me, 'that poor Jas was sweet on' – and that this seemed to be the talk of the town. It seemed also that Sheriff Parkman had tried out his theory of knives on whosoever wished to debate the matter.

'The Pony Express of gossip gallops on,' said the lawyer Briscoe. 'Well, that ain't law and that ain't evidence. They have you wrapped up nicely and you soon to be posted to perdition – far as they are concerned. We'll see, said the blind rat.'

Chapter Twenty-Two

So now I had a few days for my soul to sink into whatever abyss souls sink into when they are affrighted. Even my dreams were laced with evil happenings. The storm went west to Arkansas, went off travelling by old routes and new maybe even as far as my lost country, the shadows of my mother and my sister. I ached for a happy thought. Now the air emboldened and threads of strange gold seemed to blow through the sunlight. In my mood of fear and fright it seemed laden with all wrong prophecy, that wide high sky of fool's gold spread behind the lawyer Briscoe's new house. I longed for Thomas and John Cole, I longed for Peg, for Rosalee. I longed for all the sacred stupidity of ordinary life. What the deer feels in the second she sees the hunter with his gun I seemed to feel for long stretches of hours and days. I was poised for flight like any creature might be but where I was to flee I didn't know.

Noble ideas weren't much of a balm. The time comes when you are just what you are, without frills. You feel yourself to be so. Seventeen, eighteen years old, with a bunch of ideas about myself – but how easily, quickly all that was swept away. I thought of the whiskey I had drunk, I thought of the things I couldn't see, the events that were dark. Blundering through twisting darkness. Sometimes a glimpse of faces, sometimes a stray torch of light showing limbs and clothes, a room, a street – then darkness closing again. Black black darkness. But how wretched, how solo, how alone, in my thoughts. At the middle of all was a hurting thought that I had been the cause of everything had happened to me. I had been raised high by Thomas and John Cole but now I was pitched down to what I really was. And what I really was didn't seem to have even a mouthful of words to tell me its nature. A ragged thing of an unwanted people. I sat alone at the lawyer Briscoe's and wondered if I shrank away to nothing would I just disappear? A thing so light and worthless that the smallest breeze would carry it off, that strange light stuff that wraps a new leaf, so it rolled and tumbled in the ditches of the world.

◐

Then Peg arrived.

We were alone together in Lana Jane Sugrue's temporary quarters. Even though just a stopgap she had prettied it up as best she could. It was only a corner of a corner of the barn. Her brothers had hung some old lengths of linen for her to make a room so there was an atmosphere in it something like a teepee. Even though Peg seemed burdened by something she smiled when she saw it. She clapped her hands like a child and laughed. The happiness of just being with her pierced into me like arrows. Like knives. It was such a painful happiness because my deepest mind was telling me my legs were in the slough and I could never be sucked free from it again.

'Two nights past it was true what I said,' Peg began. 'You just slept the sleep of the innocent and when it was maybe two hours nigh midnight I could not sleep and rose and went out to the stables and got me a mule and as quiet as the quietest thing ever was I went into Paris to punish that boy.'

'Jas Jonski?'

'Ain't no way to say this excepting if I ain't saying it now, I ain't never going to sleep again, I ain't never going to hardly breathe,' she said.

'I went into Paris to punish that boy. I could see the suffering in you. It were anger carried me then. A desire that ain't to be resisted to have justice for that girl I love, justice for Winona.'

'I am Winona, here in front of you.'

'I know,' she said.

Then she drew breath.

'So I go into that wretched town and I creeping along the ways but I know because you said it that he lived back of Mr Hicks's store so I am asking a couple of jack-ass boys where that might be and then in the dark I am standing outside and I see the little light of his window and I creep through the little rose garden Mr Hicks seem to have and the roses are prickling me all the way and I gaze in the window. I don't even have a gun, I don't even have my knife, and then I am thinking what a damn fool I am and nothing to fight with and I am just on the point of going back to my mule which of course I had tethered up by the last woods and I am just on the point of spinning round on my feet and going back and getting back to Lige's and creeping back into our bed and lying along your back like only angels get to do and feeling your sweet warm body against me and then though what do I see? I see a body not warm or sweet but it be Jas Jonski strewn cross his own dank little bed and by heaven blood all round and over everything and this cold scene lit by a candle that fluttered and gasped on his table and I thought, someone has done the deed, someone they have done the work that needed to be doing. And I crept away back through the town and tried not to be seen and I was happy that boy was dead. And I rode home to you, and you never had stirred, and even when I slipped in behind you you never stirred, only let out a tiny sound.

And that my story told cold and that the proof that you never killed nobody and that the bare truth and it can be told to everyone.'

'Peg, my Peg, it a story can be told to no one, to nobody. You tell that story then it just you replaced for me and just the hangman's noose just the same and that for me would be the same, to lose you would be to lose myself. Peg, you must never tell another what you told me. Never.'

'I heard you reading the letter to John Cole and I heard what he said and I thought just since we be of no account in the world I had best be judge and jury and do the right thing which would be the thing directed to do by love.'

'Peg, you think we said enough about that? What I saying is, you think we said everything clearly enough? We sometimes say love and sometimes say like and we just together as if we both chose it without a word and if I be the half of myself you be the other half. Do you know what it is to me that you would go off in the deep dark of the night and try and fetch justice for me? Do you know how that heals me and hots my heart and makes me feel more braver than that bear that took steps to kill us in the woods? Do you know when I look on you now how my heart swells with something, with pride or something, or a feeling so big I guess mountains ain't the equal of it?'

'I guess we found each other,' she whispered, her face an inch from mine, 'I guess we did. And we weren't even looking for each other when we found each other. Ain't that strange?'

◐

Well, Peg was obliged to go back to Lige's because we thought we couldn't be turning the lawyer Briscoe's into a hotel. I gave her my señorita gun and my knife because something told me it was best to go without arms now. I was burning with a better force now. I was clearer, I was balanced like Thomas McNulty dancing, whirling, and stepping in the lost days and footlights of Grand Rapids.

But I wondered, could I live in my mother's hoop of time any more? Did I have to put my foot on the whiteman's strict straight line now? Because I didn't want anything to come round again. In earlier times in the protection of my mother I wanted that because I lived in a dress of feathers, beads, and happiness. But what could I do in a black suit of sorrow?

◐

Then of course because it couldn't be anything else to happen Frank Parkman – Sheriff Parkman – came out to the lawyer Briscoe. He was alone, without deputies, so sure of the rightful ground he stood on that he wouldn't need them. He showed a paper to the lawyer Briscoe and the lawyer Briscoe perused it and handed it back to him. This all on the new open space in front of the house, the workmen there that day looking down from the roof where they were sticking in pots. Nice new chimney pots made in New England and two weeks it took to get them down to Tennessee. There to rise proudly from the stack for evermore, hoped the lawyer Briscoe. No more depredations against things as innocent as chimney pots. In the meantime, this scrap of paper with this and that on it and my name.

The lawyer Briscoe said I would most likely have to go with Sheriff Parkman. Well, I didn't have a horse or mule so Virg Sugrue was told to rattle me in on the buggy. Anyway the lawyer Briscoe didn't intend in the general undertaking of his business to let me go alone, though Sheriff Parkman was strenuous in his speeches to try and make exactly that happen.

'Plenty of time to set her to rights,' he said. 'She don't need no lawyer just now. I just to question her on suspicion. I ain't arresting her if she so allows. If she won't come then I guess we clap the irons on her and bring her along, shouting insults against me.'

Sheriff Parkman was as devoted to his tobacco as ever.

He had extracted his little clay pipe and had stuffed it with baccy and now with a flashing lucifer he lit it. The other thing strange about him I was thinking was that way he had of laughing at everything – laughing to the point of craziness. Maybe he expected me to be frightened and folding but I was neither. Peg had brought me out clean underclothes at the behest of Rosalee and I was grateful for those starchy items. And she had brought a clean dress which just happened to be the famous yellow dress, a dress Peg could always spare, since she thought so little of it. I had taken the yellow dress with a wry laugh. Then I had my army coat as in Thomas McNulty's old coat and I had two jackets that Rosalee had sewn in the same white stuff she had made my trews and shirts out of. I would have loved to wear my trews and shirts and why was I not wearing them?

'You got to be a girl the while,' she said. 'Lige Magan said so. Did you ever see Lige when he blows? Thomas McNulty said why in hell you had to but Lige Magan kept saying it was so so I brought the damn dress. They was arguing and arguing. John Cole staggering about saying Death was to be preferred. Rosalee weeping and demanding justice of God. They just boats unmoored by the flood and they going to be broke up in the rapids by and by.'

And then I petted her the best I could and then she was gone.

So now I was decked out in that way I have described and I don't know what gods or God had given me the grace of that moment but I did not fear.

Chapter Twenty-Three

The lawyer Briscoe embraced me at the sheriff's office. He had never embraced me before and it was over quicker than the downturn of a bird's wing. I had time to notice that the paunch of his stomach was gone – that house-building had stripped the poor man of his fat, like winter strips the bear. Sheriff Parkman was not inclined to welcome him any further and the lawyer Briscoe was obliged to take leave of me.

'Send out a boy as soon as I needed,' he said to the sheriff. 'Do not fail.'

'Mr Briscoe,' said Frank Parkman flatly. He didn't use his jocular self with the lawyer Briscoe so much, I noted.

Then I was bustled down into the jail cell proper. Young Wynkle King was there with a mop and bucket cleaning up after someone had vomited. No sign of life otherwise. He was mopping away with his gun still forlornly in its holster.

'You brought her in then?' he said. He didn't say anything to me.

'Well I guess I did,' said Frank Parkman.

He told me to sit on the bench and then Wynkle King banged away off with his bucket and then Sheriff Parkman stepped back into the corridor and fetched a stool and then he set down just near me and started to fuss with his infernal pipe. He also was armed and for a moment I wondered could I get the gun from him and shoot him, quickly. But then what would be the use of that? He would be dead and I would be a murderer.

'We going to get you arraigned pretty quick, see if we don't. No sense in delaying nothing. I guess you'll hang, that's it. Judge Littlefair he sitting now next week – real convenient for you. This ain't no place to be waiting for nothing. No.'

◐

No prairie snow in Paris any time of year but it was mighty cold in that dank place. Twice I heard the voice of Thomas McNulty shouting in the office – then both times it was followed by laughter. I guess Sheriff Parkman didn't want me to see anyone but the lawyer Briscoe. Rosalee Bouguereau sent in delights and for some reason Sheriff Parkman was content to let me have them. Chief among these was her rabbit stew. Otherwise I don't know who was to feed me. Mopping maybe was Wynkle

King's only domestic skill and Sheriff Parkman thought eggs were born in a pan.

The lawyer Briscoe was busy lining up his arguments and finding witnesses. If I were to say he seemed to grow more gloomy over this work I would be speaking against the promise I made to myself, to be hopeful and bet for a good outcome. I was wondering and wondering about Judge Littlefair. Surely I had robbed Tennyson's own gun from under his nose but contrariwise I had Peg for an ally. Was he going to hang Peg's friend? I didn't know.

The day of the trial came on quick icy feet. At length I was led over to the courthouse which I and Jas Jonski had idly passed many times. Sheriff Parkman paid me the compliment of having me in chains. The townsfolk seemed mighty pleased to gather to watch the show.

All was noise and to-ing and fro-ing and even caterwauling in the courtroom. I was brought up like a dead soul from the underground holding cell. I saw the spread of faces and the bright staring eyes. Then in came the judge from a door at the back, Aurelius Littlefair in his black funereal suit, his face hair bristling like that wild boar I had eaten in pie form. The courtroom was cold and sweaty in one, people all padded out in big coats. It was just the yellow dress for me and I don't know why but I felt no cold. The atmosphere of eager faces and excited chatter reminded me of Grand Rapids days, when as a little girl I would stand at the side of the stage and peep out at the audience, ear cocked to the strange seaside roar it made, as if it were a gigantic shell held to my ear.

I knew Jas Jonski had been much liked and no one knew me hardly in the town, except those who now seemed to be my enemies. Now the jury filed in and looked at me as if ashamed but of course not ashamed – sideways glances like prospective lovers make. Not much love likely, I was thinking. I was struggling in my thoughts not to be what they thought they saw, a skinny Indian in a ragged dress.

My lovely Thomas McNulty and John Cole were ranged along the nearest seats, and Lige, and Rosalee. Thomas didn't stint to wave to me. John Cole I could see, still thin as a prisoner, was constraining himself from rushing forward. There were six militia men lining the left wall, and the court bailiffs were armed with pistols and rifles, looking fearsome, like they were on the cusp of a mighty battle. I knew poor Thomas would have feared so mightily to come near that place, carrying after his own incarceration for evermore the seared soul of the felon. Rosalee had scrubbed the three men raw and all were shaved except Lige, who I could see in my mind's eye begging clemency for his moustache. Thomas McNulty looked young, his old fled self of beauty and youth part redeemed by Rosalee's shaving, and the shadow of the court, his cheeks sallow as a moon, his long grey hair trimmed back and darkened by pomade. John Cole and his narrow Indian face, so quiet, so calm, a cover for the rapids running through his mind, I did not doubt.

The jury a mixture of the rough and well-to-do – older men in older coats, and young men calling out to the fashions of Knoxville, Memphis, and Nashville. Cavalry trews without the yellow stripe. Ferocious haircuts from the German barber down the square.

Judge Littlefair's clerk took his court in order and tried to extinguish the fire of talk. Soon enough it was just a smoking pyre. The lawyer Briscoe sat beside me, and I thought Aurelius Littlefair might hide his contempt for him, but he fair did not, to judge by the first fierce look at this man he detested. Who had signed that document of death for Colonel Purton and likely other crimes against the old Confederacy.

Aurelius Littlefair now spoke to the jury as though they were the fond beneficiaries of his thoughts. The jurymen stared at him respectfully, eagerly, wanting to understand whatever he said to them. Judge Littlefair asked the lawyer Briscoe how I pled to the charge of murder in the first degree, and the lawyer Briscoe said Not Guilty. The room surged with suppressed reactions, the clerk wielded his invisible whip to schtum them. The legal proem of the offence was read out and the nature of it illuminated and the possible outcomes and decisions and their responsibilities explained to the jury. Then the prosecuting lawyer, a tall bent man with a gold tie-pin and patent shoes, with a nice soft face, gave his speech. He told us what he intended to prove and who he would call and he was in no doubt that we had the guilty party here in court. I was sorry that I looked at Thomas's face just then, because it was a blushing face of suffering.

When the lawyer Briscoe spoke, the words seemed to me to scrape along the floor and reach the jury exhausted and pale, but that might just have been my crazy notion. He spoke well of me and denied the charge and said he would call witnesses would back him up and that that would be that, no doubt, and they would understand that in no manner could I have committed the crime and indeed it must be laid at the door of some person unknown at present. I had never seen the lawyer Briscoe 'in action'. He was very much the actor, Mr Noone in Grand Rapids would have been well pleased with him. With his roundy phrases and his grave looks. I thought the flat stomach suited him well except he still wore a black velvet waistcoat made to accommodate it, so it hung from him like an extra skin.

But all still might have been well, I didn't know. I was just a girl there in enemy territory, that's what it felt like. When the handsome prosecutor spoke against me, he sounded so certain even I quailed in my seat, as if indeed a person with so foul a deed like a weevil in my soul. John Cole was called to speak for me, and prettily he did so. He could have said everything he needed in a John Cole look, instead he knew he had to expand his usual succinct thoughts. He gave them when asked all my short history and who I was and how he hoped someday to send me up to Dartmouth College where an Indian might 'larn something rare', as he put it.

Then Peg was called. She must have been kept in the corridor. She was wearing an egregious pinny she favoured, I knew not why. The big doors were screeched open by the bailiffs and in she came, small and frightened-looking. And I was shocked to see her not only because I feared for her but also because it was difficult for me to look at her at any time without a kind of shock. All the same I was watching the face of Aurelius Littlefair to see how he would be responding. He gave the mere hint of a grimace but otherwise remained separate and austere from our occasions.

The lawyer Briscoe asked Peg his questions and she spoke in her simple, strangely cheerful voice. She recounted her tale that she had seen me fall asleep just after nightfall and that I had not woken again till morning. The prosecutor pointed out to her that she couldn't have known that, since she had been asleep herself. How far was it to the town? Could a person take a mule out quietly from the stable? Were there dogs to bark on Lige Magan's place? Weren't you a dear close friend of the accused and bound to speak well for her? Was she not an Indian like me, and were Indians not renowned for their duplicity? Did not the Declaration of Independence expressly refer to her sort as 'the merciless Indian savages whose known rule of warfare is an undistinguished destruction of all ages, sexes, and conditions'? Peg said she didn't know, she had not heard that. The jury looked deeply impressed by her savagery nonetheless and as they knew no Indians in Henry County, were likely very glad anew the Chickasaw had been removed years past. Then Peg was removed too, having answered all her questions with a kind of sweet demureness.

So then came the two boys who said they 'seen an Injun girl' and spoke to her and answered her question about where Mr Hicks kept his dry-goods store, and when the prosecutor asked if the Indian girl was in the courtroom, they said *yea*, and pointed at me.

Then the important evidence of Sheriff Parkman was itemised, and he mentioned the fact that he knew

I carried a knife in my boot, and that I bore a great grudge against his friend Mr Jonski, and refused to marry him, and had tried to lower Mr Jonski in the eyes of the world by stories and lies, and that such was my hatred, it was no news to the sheriff that I would have killed Jas Jonski. The judge enquired of him had he seen me that night near or around the body, and Sheriff Parkman was not such a barefaced liar as to say he had. But he said he knew of no one who would want Jas Jonski more dead than me, and that all his dealings with me had shown him that I was ill-tempered, savage, and strange.

Throughout this I was obliged to keep my gaze averted from Thomas, John, Lige, and Rosalee, all of who, maybe even Rosalee, may have been considering an attempt on the lives of everyone there and a quick gallop down to Mexico.

This all took but two hours of the court's time. The court clerks were kept busy writing it all down. I thought of the documents maybe copied out and stored in the lawyer Briscoe's records, for another assistant to find, and ask him, well, who was Winona Cole, what happened to her? And the lawyer Briscoe going to the cabinet for his whiskey . . .

The prosecutor made a brief little parley, very satisfied, he said, of my plain and irrefutable guilt, the lawyer

Briscoe tried a few Latin quotes, he was convinced of my innocence, assured of it, and he knew the jury would be too.

He was wrong on that occasion. The jury was sent away for a little and came back so quickly they caught out the members of the public who had strolled off to stretch their legs.

Aurelius Littlefair gazed down upon me, as if to say, this will teach you for stealing that Spencer rifle. This will teach you for stealing Peg away. Just for a moment before the head juryman spoke, I had a crazy little hope he might say something good. How do you find? said Aurelius Littlefair. Guilty, said the man, looking shocked by his own importance.

The judge heard the decision of the jury calmly and he opined that I was to be hung at the earliest convenience of the county executioner, viz. the following week.

I didn't shiver and shake. I heard nothing and everything. I wondered suddenly what it would be like to feel the noose around my neck. I thought a little thing like my neck would break quickly. I thought of the soldier hacking at my mother. It was just a noble thing what happened to us in America. We were the lost people of Turtle Island. Death was our door to paradise, no doubt. If my sister had been obliged to go before me, I could go too. All the same I knew I was crying quietly. I heard the sobs of Thomas McNulty. I kept my hands in the lap of the yellow dress.

Many of the public present were cheering, calling, laughing. With a definitive look of *There now, Briscoe*, the judge rose from his chair and vanished through the wall like a ghost in a story.

Chapter Twenty-Four

Sheriff Parkman was very excited by the verdict and when he brought me back down to the cells it was out with the stool again from the corridor and settling himself down by me as if we were old friends.

He was just like an actor who had come off stage. Well, there had been applause. He was beaming and elated. In balance I thought this was a worse punishment than the verdict. I looked at him through other eyes. I was another Winona now, a new one. A condemned person, a girl, a boy. I could sense the fear trying to reach me, trying to arrive. Go back, go back, I cried in my thoughts, like the yardwoman driving back the hens with her spears and shields of grain. Fear, fear. Trying to touch me with its poisonous fingers, just like Jas Jonski. I thought, neither will reach me, ever again. I love my Thomas, my John, my Lige, my Rosalee, my Tennyson, my immaculate Peg.

'You don't remember what happened in the livery, do you?' said Frank Parkman, foaming with enthusiasm. 'I wonder why you don't,' he said, as if we had been discussing that for a time and he was just continuing on from that topic. 'I don't know if I ever had such a great friend as I had in Jas Jonski. A boy that meant no harm, that was full of the joys of life. He were a playful critter, a man after my own heart.'

'Do you mean,' I said, 'when I spoke to you and you thought I was a boy and you asked if you could kiss me?'

It must have been the devil made me say it. I knew he wasn't one of the souls would be easy in themselves and know their own minds and hearts. No. Well, whatever made me say it, he kept his head down for a full minute, staring at the ground, not a trace of a reaction in his face, as if I had crushed the joy of the verdict out of him. His face was dark because the cell was dark but I could still read him like a set of awkward numbers.

'You a varmint, ain't you?' he said. '*Merciless savages*, that what the old declaration called you. That why we fought *that* war. So varmints like you could be took off the world like the rats and the wolves you be.'

Then he laughed quietly to himself like he truly appreciated his own words. All in balance again, his sense of joy in things quickly restored. I felt some understanding of him, in a distant far-off way. He was not much more than a boy in a big man's job. Sheriff. The going away of Sheriff Flynn had brought him into the realm of his dreams. The troubles that afflicted Sheriff Flynn had only been a boon to another man's rise, and it was curious to me still how Sheriff Flynn had just walked out of my story. It was like the river closing over a drowning head, once down it is gone forever. I remembered the kindness and impulse to good of that gone sheriff, how he had surprised us all with his speeches of justice and right. A ragged group of listeners at a brokedown Tennessee tobacco farm. If you got to kill the Indians, I thought, this was the best thing put in our place. Men like him, Americans. But not so much like this boy. All smiling and lonesome in his heart. Then he struck his lucifer off its tinderbox in his manly gesture and a yellow globe of fire and light was suspended a moment in the dank air and then vanished. In its place was a suspended remnant of false light and then the fumes of smoke coming out of him like an engine. He laughed again, even though he had said nothing and I had said nothing.

'Well,' he said at length, 'I won't be giving you anywhere in the world to be saying *that* to people, because you going to be hanged, missy. I going to watch you being hanged. The whole town loves a hanging. Aurelius Littlefair, he was the proper judge now to tend to you. You think you so mighty high doing all the numbers for the lawyer Briscoe. He yesterday's man now. Look at you, missy, with your black hair and your dirty yellow dress and your dirty old coat and clothes. I don't know what I thought you was and I don't know why I thought to kiss you.'

Now Wynkle King came down and got himself a stool and now he was as if 'proper deputy' to Frank Parkman, sitting cosy side by side. If I could have cut my legs off not to be so near them, I would. I was wishing I had my trews and not that yellow dress. My legs were bare and I could feel the downy hairs on them stiffen and turn away from those two boys. If he wanted to talk about rats then that was what they seemed to me. But they were rats in the bloom of power.

'This the girl that poor Jas Jonski wanted,' he said to Wynkle King. 'Can you credit it? And that killed him for his trouble. Well, well, didn't I tell you?'

'You did say something about it,' said Wynkle King, and laughed at his own wit. Yes, Wynkle King chuckled, he was a chuckler, like the lawyer Briscoe, but with a different effect.

'She don't remember what happened to her in my old livery, no, she don't,' said Sheriff Parkman.

'What happen there?' said Wynkle King, with true interest.

'You don't remember, do you?' he said to me again. 'I not meaning that time you mention and I will be obliged if you say nothing about *that*.' And he laughed. Wynkle King wasn't following him there and I said nothing. If Frank Parkman was inclined to love a man I would not judge him. I had Thomas and John Cole as proof of that.

Then Frank Parkman leaned in closer, signalling to Wynkle King to lean in also. As if the world was listening and he must be intimate, friendly.

'Don't you remember that time when in former days I held your shoulders and Jas Jonski, well, he had his fun with you? And we was laughing and just having such a time, and drinking, and you was drinking, oh yes, sirree. And you was saying, Oh, oh, Jas, don't do that, and we knew what you really meant.'

Frank Parkman broke out into furious laughter, so much so that Wynkle King jumped in fright on his stool. Wynkle King didn't laugh. In fact he went very pale and looked suddenly sick, as if he might add in a minute to his bucket chores.

Well I had my answer to my own mystery at last. Here it was, from the horse's mouth. I didn't feel shame in that moment. I felt a conflagrating sense of rightness, like an equation coming out unexpectedly right. I thought, by heavens, they can hang me now but they won't be hanging a guilty soul. They'll be hanging a free soul. *We hold these truths to be self-evident, that all men are created equal. Life, Liberty.* I didn't think there was much to do except to be hanged. I didn't believe the lawyer Briscoe would prosper with the appeal he had promised, not as long as Aurelius Littlefair was looking down on us from his dais. He had burned the lawyer Briscoe's house and he wouldn't falter to hang his Injun girl. Who was to say I hadn't killed Jas Jonski, no one and nothing, except this close-sitting laughing boy, Frank Parkman. I might have killed Jas Jonski. If Frank Parkman had made that speech to me before, and I had known the truth of my own experience in the world, in that tone of mockery or even not in that tone, I might have considered it only just that I shoot Jas Jonski. I was with the Saxons on that, ref. the lawyer Briscoe. Penalty of death. But I hadn't known and had been so long in my time of fog drifting sere and dark across my thoughts I had at length taken the fog for sunlight. Now the fog was dispersed and the true wide country behind was revealed, like lovely Tennessee when spring shakes out its hair and widens its arms and stretches. And there was a whip of terror in his words but also the putting down of a whip. I thought, if I were a great lion or a bear or even a wolf, since he had called me wolf, just as my mother had been called, I could put my paws around these laughing boys and bite off their heads. I was thinking even now could I gather all my force – not to escape but to tear them from the world?

'Yes, you going to be hanged, sure enough,' said Frank Parkman, knocking the little black snag of burnt tobacco from his pipe bowl onto the floor, having smoked all the while through, 'you was seen in town that night, two boys seen you, missy, that was what will hang you, yes, sirree – even though,' and here he paused like the excellent tragedian he possibly could have been – 'we know it ain't you killed Jas Jonski neither.'

Now we were two faces staring at his face, both me and Wynkle taken by surprise.

'We know?' Wynkle King asked. 'How you mean?'

'You remember,' Sheriff Parkman said to me, his silver badge rattling tinnily as he leaned in even closer, 'that time you liked to remind me of, when you come so swanky into the livery, like a goddamn little prince? – you remember there was a black horse there, belonged to Jas Jonski's ma? And I said to you, I don't know why she come by that horse all the way from Nashville and not by the train or the stage? Why, the reason was, turned out, that poor woman as mad as a newborn foal, she living in that great old place in Nashville, Tennessee Asylum, and she always sneaking out to come see her son, causing ructions and searches with torchlight, like a good mother. But she don't like no son of hers going marrying no Injun. Why, missy, it was savages like you killed her grandmother, Jas told me, just took her and cut off her nose and generally hurt her till she dead. Out there in Nebraska Territory as was. Now Jas Jonski writes to her and says he fixing to marry you even though you done refuse his plea, and he going to write to you. I mean, missy, his ma thinking, why would a civilised boy do that? Write to you, when he can have you any hour of the day and any day of the month. Just have you and get his pleasure off you and by God there ain't no need to go marrying scum like you.'

I was staring at him, staring. Wynkle King was too. Wynkle King was hearing all this as a new speech, I could tell. But his bladder must have been twitching at him too, because he suddenly leaped up, did that little dance that children do when they need to piss, and went quickly away. Sheriff Parkman didn't even glance at him. But he edged closer yet another few inches – I could feel his breath on my face – maybe glad of the new privacy.

'So she sneaks away out of the asylum yet another time,' said Frank Parkman, with a sort of delight, 'and sets off again on some horse she finds and creeps across Tennessee, counting no doubt the miles by the sombre reckoning of the owls, and then all sere and worn she arrives in Paris, the country has eaten into her bones, into her face, she only a ghost,' he said, 'and then she goes to the abode of her dear beloved son and in the firm belief and as an act of favour, to release him she believes from his great error and raise him into the realms of freedom, she stabs him, stabs him and stabs him, those twenty counted times. Then by heavens she opens his chest with her knife and takes out his heart, the heart of her own son, and she cooks it, there on the little trestle stove he kept to warm his coffee, and she ate it. All just for his sake, all just for his sake – as she told me herself.'

I heard a faint scuffling in the shadows, but kept my eyes on Parkman.

'So – I'm coming in to see what's afoot,' said Frank Parkman, 'though if ever a man had eyes to see such things I'm a Dutch. I never seen nothing so sad nor strange. I swear to you, missy. I never did. I hope never to see it again. So I bring that poor woman away and clean her up a little, listening all the while to her chatter, how Jas was free now and he would never see hell, no, no, he would be a gold angel lifted into heaven, and hadn't she done him such motherly service, and now she could die herself a woman contented with her mercy and her deeds. Then I bring her into the terrible old building of the asylum and she's put in her jacket and all is well, and I feel I done my duty too by Jas, by saving his mother from the gallows. So I get a boy to send a message to Colonel Purton, *Well, Purton,* or such like, *Jas Jonski been killed, I reckon I know who it was, it was that there Winona Cole, the evil Injun girl*. Yes, I brought that poor crazy woman back to Nashville, took me a whole long night and day of coaxing and riding along just inch by inch – got her back in her quarters. They was so glad to see that prodigal woman.'

I sat there saying nothing.

'Where's that Wynkle?' said Frank Parkman looking round behind him, and then seeing Wynkle standing there, suddenly, an oily stain on the darkness. 'You back, Wynkle?'

Wynkle King trod dolefully out of the shadows and sat on his stool as if maybe nothing had changed – he had taken the story of my ravishment in his stride after all – but I wondered if I could see a strange stirring in him. His face twitching with thought.

'You saying we going to fix to hang this girl but you know some crazy woman did it?' he said suddenly, with the force of a tree stump busting free in a flooded river. 'You saying that?'

I saw Frank Parkman's face flinch with a sort of misery. It was clear he had not meant to be overheard. Then he gathered himself, he tightened himself, almost recklessly, in a monstrous effort to avert disaster.

'You think we can hang Jas Jonski's mother?' he said, like this reaction of Wynkle King's was a great surprise to him, and even something to offend his sense of rightness, as any man might agree. 'A poor afflicted woman and the mother of my friend? Someone got to hang for it. Why not this girl?'

Again a silence. In the silence I saw a mouse cross the cell floor, from right to left, as if it had not a care in the world, and showing not a grain of interest in us.

'Because that ain't right,' said Wynkle King, with all the innocent tone of a child. With a father like his maybe he knew what he was talking about. His father who had also eaten human flesh.

'You never had a good thought, Wynkle,' said Frank Parkman, almost humorously. 'Don't have a good thought now.'

'I ain't allowing you – I just ain't letting you. I just ain't going along with it. You think I such a wretch? You don't know me, Frank Parkman.'

'I know you well enough, you a creeping little Confederate backwater son-of-a-bitch.'

'Why, who you, the emperor of Nashville?'

Wynkle King had gotten to his feet and the stool went skittering along the cold floor. It was a stool of bare wood, you could see the whittling in it. Sheriff Parkman twisted round as he rose too, so he would be square on to Wynkle King. He dropped his precious pipe and now he trod on it by accident, crushing it to dust, adding to his rising fury. I was sitting there amazed. I didn't move a hair. I was inclined to put my face in my hands, I knew not why, but I kept them fastened to my skirts. I had heard such terrible things but they had been of the past and now here was a terrible thing brewing right in front of me, inches from my knees. Wynkle King couldn't help himself, his hand was on his gun and then he was lifting the gun from the holster like it was a great weight. It was like his arm wasn't able to lift that gun hardly.

'You never going to shoot no goddamn sheriff,' said the sheriff, so greatly offended and amazed. 'You never.'

As if to prove this to its conclusion Frank Parkman got his gun out clumsily enough. He lofted the polished gun to the level of Wynkle King's chest.

'You never going to shoot no sheriff,' he said again, and then there was a violent bang, that bang you get from a gun fired in a small room, that might tear out your eardrums, so the room is echoing with an enormous sound. Frank Parkman's gun dipped down and then he tried to raise it again, he was struggling so from the force of the bullet into him somewhere. Wynkle King had shot him, but with his last seed of strength Frank Parkman fired, he fired, and I felt the bullet burn into me.

◐

I woke in the great yard of the penitentiary. I knew exactly where I was. I had never been there before but I knew it somehow. A huge grey mass of a building reared up behind me. I was dressed in the clothes of a Lakota fighting man. How happy I was to see them on my chest and legs. A great crowd of my people were before me. It was curious to me that my mother was there but I accepted that as strangely possible. I was surprised to find I must have lived a thousand moons. She looked so like me, not as a shadow, but an actual living person. It was wonderful to me how she smiled at me. Caught-His-Horse-First, the great chief, smiled too, as if all his efforts to get me back had at last been successful. Things can turn out so well, just when you least expect it. There were many soldiers there, and two Gatling guns set up, with troopers bent over them like men at big telescopes.

But the people were all talking at the same time, these beautiful Lakota, and some were very old and some were very young. Caught-His-Horse-First was wearing a long wide bib of beads down his chest, it went right down to the ground and swept about when he moved.

'Are you alive, uncle?' I said to him. 'I thought you had been killed.'

'I wasn't killed,' he said, 'but it might still happen. We don't know. We were waiting for you to come up.'

'Come up from where?'

'From the ground. You were under the ground, walking. Now you are here.'

'My mother,' I said to my mother, 'I was so little when the soldiers came, I want to tell you how I admire you and I am so glad you are famous for your courage. Without that I could not live.'

'You could live without it,' she said, 'but it is better to have it.'

This was all being said in Lakota, I was dizzy from the joy of speaking it. I thought, I never thought I would see them again, how wonderful it is, how wonderful.

'Look, Ojinjintka,' she said, 'the time has come now, and you must stand there and then when I call your name, you must run towards us and then cross the wall.'

'But how can I cross such a high wall?'

'I will be there to help you, with your sister.'

So that seemed all right and I understood what she wanted. There were maybe two hundred souls between me and the high wall. The first ones lay down flat on the ground, the next ones were a little higher, and so on and so on, till there was a sort of sideways sea of backs – lovely Lakota backs, and all alive – from me to the wall. And at the wall now I could see, yes, my mother, but also my sister, I was excited to see her, they held each other's hands, the two women, facing each other, like they meant to lift me in the cradle their hands made, how beautiful she was, my sister, and alive, then my mother called my name, *Ojinjintka, Ojinjintka,* and then I knew what to do, I knew, I didn't know how, I started to run, and I stepped on the first people, and then as I crossed their backs of course I was getting higher and higher off the ground, and then I was running at speed, my heart like a hummingbird beating its wings, and I reached for the outstretched hands of my mother and sister.

◐

When I woke – when I woke again – I saw Thomas McNulty sitting at the side of the little bed in my dark room at Lige's farm. I thought his face was raised in pensive mood but then I saw that he was sleeping. Not for the first time in the story of the world a motherly person had fallen asleep by the bed of their child.

At the end of the narrow bed lay Peg, a small figure curled, as warm as a wolf. She wore the ragged yellow dress. Her only blanket was the moonlight.

That the world was strange and lost was not in argument. That there was no place to stand on the earth that was not perilous was just the news of every moment.

That I had souls that loved me and hearts that watched over me was a truth self-evident to hold.

The author is indebted to very many books in the making of this story, in particular *Indian Boyhood* by Charles A. Eastman (Ohiyesa), McClure, Phillips & Co., 1902.

Also by Sebastian Barry

Days Without End

Winner of the Costa Book of the Year Award 2016

After signing up for the US army in the 1850s, barely seventeen, Thomas McNulty and his brother-in-arms, John Cole, fight in the Indian Wars and the Civil War. Having both fled terrible hardships, their days are now vivid and filled with wonder, despite the horrors they both see and are complicit in. But when a young Indian girl crosses their path, Thomas and John must decide on the best way of life for them all in the face of dangerous odds.

'Epic, lyrical and constantly surprising . . . a rich and satisfying novel.' *Independent*

'Humorous, compassionate, true . . . It is the stern, glorious music of a great novel.' *Irish Times*

'A beautiful, savage, life-affirming masterpiece.' Donal Ryan, *Observer* Books of the Year

'A true leftfield wonder . . . A violent, superbly lyrical western offering a sweeping vision of America in the making.' Kazuo Ishiguro

Also by Sebastian Barry

The Temporary Gentleman

Ghana, 1957: Jack McNulty, a former UN observer, sits in his lodgings contemplating his return to Ireland, and the life he has led. He has worked around the world and seen extraordinary things, yet Jack's memories are dominated by his tumultuous marriage back in Sligo in the 1920s to Mai Kirwan, a great beauty with a vivid mind. But Mai is elusive, mysterious and troubled, and in time she slipped from his grasp. *The Temporary Gentleman* is a novel about one man's attempt to free himself from the savage realities of his past.

'A book that leaves the reader bruised long after the final page has been, regretfully, turned.' John Harding, *Daily Mail*

'Almost as if good writing might have the power to save a marriage or contain the secret of happiness . . . rare and heart-breaking.' Kate Kellaway, *Observer*

'One's heart leaps into one's mouth and stays there . . . exhilarating.' Charlotte Moore, *Spectator*

Also by Sebastian Barry

On Canaan's Side

Longlisted for the Man Booker Prize

Dublin, 1918. At the end of the First World War, Lilly Bere and her sweetheart Tadg are forced to flee Ireland for America. They plan to marry and forge a new life together, in the hope that their past will not catch up with them.

Seven decades later, Lilly, mourning the loss of her grandson, tries to make sense of her own life and the lives of the people she has loved. At once epic and intimate, *On Canaan's Side* is a novel of memory, war, family ties and love.

'A marvel of empathy and tact.' Joseph O'Neill

'Imbued with sorrow, joy, tenderness and also moments of great humour, *On Canaan's Side* is a luminously beautiful story.' *Independent on Sunday*

'A powerful meditation on love, war, the strength of family bonds and the unfathomable instincts of friendship.' *Scotland on Sunday*

Also by Sebastian Barry

The Secret Scripture

Shortlisted for the Man Booker Prize 2008
Winner of the Costa Book of the Year Award 2008
Irish Book Awards Novel of the Year

The mental hospital where psychiatrist Dr Grene works is about to shut down, and he sets about investigating the history of his patient Roseanne. She was committed there as a young woman and now – her records long lost – is nearing her hundredth birthday. At the same time, Roseanne is looking back on the tragedies and passions of her life through a secret journal: her turbulent childhood in rural 1930s Ireland, and the subsequent marriage which she believed would finally bring her happiness. When Dr Grene finally uncovers the circumstances of her arrival at the hospital, it leads to a secret that will shock them both.

'An astonishing story, told with sadness and grace, full of gleaming images . . . the rich, enduring voice of Roseanne is remarkable.' *The Times*

Also by Sebastian Barry

A Long Long Way

Shortlisted for the Man Booker Prize 2005

One of the most vivid and realised characters of recent fiction, Willie Dunne is the innocent hero of Sebastian Barry's highly acclaimed novel. Leaving Dublin to fight for the Allied cause as a member of the Royal Dublin Fusiliers, he finds himself caught between the war playing out on foreign fields and that festering at home, waiting to erupt with the Easter Rising. Profoundly moving, intimate and epic, *A Long Long Way* charts and evokes a terrible coming of age, one too often written out of history.

'Unsurpassed in First World War fiction. A small master-piece.' *Independent*

'The story grips, shocks and saddens; but most importantly refuses to be forgotten.' *The Times*

'A stunning achievement . . . Barry has written one of the most moving fictional accounts of war that surely must rank alongside those real-life testimonies of Owen and Sassoon.' *Sunday Tribune*

Also by Sebastian Barry

Annie Dunne

Annie Dunne and her cousin Sarah live and work on a small farm in a remote and beautiful part of Wicklow in late 1950s Ireland. All about them the old green roads are being tarred, cars are being purchased, a way of life is about to disappear. Then, when Annie's nephew and his wife are set to go to London to find work, their two small children, a little boy and his older sister, are brought down to spend the summer with their grand-aunt, and a summer of adventure, pain, delight and ultimately epiphany unfolds in this poignant and exquisitely told story of innocence, loss and reconciliation.

'A masterpiece . . . the novel takes on a compelling emotional depth and holds you in its grip.' Colm Tóibín

'Unsentimental and exact, like clear glass.' *The Times*

'There are beautiful passages of writing . . . the closest that fine writing can ever come to prayer.' *Irish Times*

faber

Also by Sebastian Barry

The Whereabouts of Eneas McNulty

Following the end of the First World War, Eneas McNulty joins the British-led Royal Irish Constabulary. With all those around him becoming soldiers of a different kind, however, it proves to be the defining decision of his life when, having witnessed the murder of a fellow RIC policeman, he is wrongly accused of identifying the executioners. With a sentence of death passed over him he is forced to flee Sligo, his friends, family and beloved girl, Viv.

What follows is the story of this flight, his subsequent wanderings, and the haunting pull of home that always afflicts him. Tender, witty, troubling and tragic, *The Whereabouts of Eneas McNulty* tells the secret history of a lost man.

'A powerful, unique book, Sebastian Barry's language is utterly new and quite magnificent.' *Roddy Doyle*

'It's the language that seduces you – elegant, comical, tragical, musical. It's a symphony of a novel and you'll sing along and wander with Eneas into the next century.' *Frank McCourt*

faber